RITE OF *Spring*

RITE OF *Spring*

A Novel

Virginia Weir

Chapter 1

She looked as though she had attempted to dress appropriately for an audition: white blouse, black slacks and one of those tapestry vests that were still popular in the cheap stores of the Mission District. Herminda Matta could have been anywhere from 15 to 20 years old and small, no more than five feet tall, perhaps 100 pounds. There was a line of sweat on her upper lip, as there was on most visitors who were afraid to park on the steep incline and instead hiked up Hill Street to his flat. Beyond her, on the sidewalk, Gerald saw her bassoon case strapped with bungee cords to a luggage tote.

Gerald didn't know what registered on his face—incredulity? distaste? John said he wore a perpetual look of scorn on his face, even when resting, and Gerald felt bad about this—he didn't *intend* to look that way.

But this girl was looking him up and down, too. "That's *Er*, like *er-ror*," she said, extending her hand, "and *Minda*, like *mean*. Herminda." She rolled her r's.

Gerald almost laughed out loud.

The voice was cheerful enough, but her face was hard, testy. Not a beautiful face by any accounting—long and brown and thin. Her chin was almost pointed, with a little scar on the end, and one side of her face was the slightest bit heavier than the other. Long black hair fell over her shoulders, cut in a shag style with two hideous wings of bangs swirling off her forehead.

It was her eyes, however, that kept him from laughing—huge and dark in the angular face. An intelligence in those eyes.

"Herminda," Gerald repeated, and shook her thin hand, looking past her again to the luggage cart. "Gerald Poulin."

"It's the easiest way to get around," she explained, following his gaze. She hoisted the cart up the steps and into the flat. From the looks of the battered case, Gerald suspected her bassoon might be one of those pieces of black plastic rented for high school bands.

"You brought your own music, I hope."

She nodded quickly and waited in the front room while Gerald went into the kitchen to make sure the chairs were set up. He opened the blinds when he came back into the living room and the room brightened, the April mid-afternoon sun reflecting off the white clapboard houses down the hill.

Herminda stood awkwardly by the sliding glass door and unstrapped her bassoon case. "Kind of a white place you got," she said, glancing around the apartment.

That was, he supposed, a correct assessment, since the living room was almost entirely white: white sofa, thick white carpet, three white walls (the fourth was a built-in bookcase made of walnut), and a glass coffee table with a square white plexiglass base. Jeanette, his aunt, had loaned Gerald the money to buy the flat almost 15 years ago, and when she died he'd received her white leather sofa. The rest of the room was arranged to remind him of other friends—the art deco lamp made of an old tin clarinet from Stephen, and the African masks from a trip John had taken a couple of years ago.

The small redwood deck was encircled in potted plants, including one huge saguaro cactus that loomed over the other foliage like an intruder. Past the deck there was a northeast view of Dolores Park and downtown San Francisco, the Bay Bridge glimmering beyond.

"A nice view," she said stiffly, turning to him.

"Thank you. I've set up a stand in the kitchen. Shall we begin?"

She picked up her case and followed him into the kitchen. Gerald had pushed the round teak breakfast table into the corner and set up two chairs in the middle of the room with a music stand in front of her chair and his seat off to the side.

"I'll just give you a few moments to warm up," he said, smiling mechanically, "then I'd like to hear the music you've chosen." He took a cigarette for his wait from the blue bowl on the table. Her black patent shoes, he noticed, were bent from wear at the balls of the feet. From what he'd seen so far, this wouldn't take long.

Gerald looked around his living room and felt, primarily, satisfied. He had lived alone in this small old building on Hill Street for 22 years, renting and then buying it when the flat became available. A long time—as long as he'd been in the Symphony. He caught his reflection off the sliding glass door as he lit his one cigarette of the day, a slight, 51-year old man, and for a second (only a second) he wondered what this girl thought of him. What hair he had was red, and he wore a toupee, which may or may not have been obvious, since the shade of red didn't exactly match the hair below it. That day he was wearing his customary outfit: pressed gray slacks and a yellow oxford shirt open two buttons at the top.

From the couch, he smoked and listened to Herminda assemble her bassoon (he hadn't bothered to see what kind it was), adjust her seat strap (he heard the buckle clank against the chair leg) and straighten her sheet music. There was the slight swooshing sound as she blew air into the bocal to warm it up, a litany of familiar sounds made suddenly strange when heard from another room. Gerald could not imagine what or how she would play and was already formulating how he would tell her he really was unable to take on any more students, to practice hard, etcetera.

He had to give her credit for persistence. She'd called the Symphony office to get the name of the first bassoonist, and when she found his number was unlisted she cajoled an address out of the secretary, came to his apartment and left a barely legible note asking about the possibility of lessons—signed, "Sincerely, Herminda Matta." *Her Mind*, he'd thought, deciphering the name, and smiled. What kind of a name was that? Gerald had been curious and, over the phone, with pots and pans banging and someone scolding in Spanish in the background, he'd agreed against his better judgment to give her an audition.

He heard her begin. She was probably nervous, and what was supposed to be a low note came out as a squeak before the horn begin to resonate. It wasn't a piece of cheap plastic; he could tell that much from the living room. He listened as she took her time with the C scale, giving a whole note to each tone. She played the scale faster, then arpeggios, then low F followed by high F. Gerald was getting curious, and after a few more minutes of warm-up, he rose from the couch and went into the kitchen.

In the bottom register of the instrument, her jaw dropped low on the reed, her thin face would have looked painfully distorted and probably frightening to anyone who wasn't familiar with the bassoon. With the instrument angled across her body, they formed a kind of italic X. The horn was a Fox, he noted, obviously used from the light scratches in the reddish-brown wood on the end, but still one of the higher-end models.

"Ready?" Gerald asked, and sat down in the chair next to her before she could reply. A reed carrier, self-fashioned from a box for throat lozenges lined and with felt was on the music stand, three reeds resting in it like little red-handled doll brooms.

He wondered what she would play for him.

Herminda pursed her lips together tightly, and without giving him a glance she set up a short solo from a battered exercise book that he recognized and adjusted her seat strap, nestling the base of the bassoon in its cup so that the weight of her body on the strap supported the weight of the instrument. She moistened the reed with her mouth to loosen up the cane, then twisted it onto the bocal.

She nodded and squinted at the page of music, tapping her foot to come in at the middle of a measure. A squeak. "*Shit,*" she said, just under her breath.

Why did she choose this solo, beginning on low F, requiring a very soft reed to come in properly? he wondered. "I'll try again," she said, and took a deep breath and closed her eyes. She was annoyed, and apparently the little rush of irritation helped to get the first low note out.

Gerald watched her move through the five-minute solo and tried to keep from staring by deliberately breaking his gaze every now and then and focusing on a small scuff on the floor. Her small hands were incredibly strong. From the corner of his eye, he watched her splayed fingers on the horn, the nails clean and uneven. They seemed too slender to completely cover the air holes, but did, somehow. He knew and had played this piece many times—it was a standard in the big gray book—but something about the way she was playing made it sound new.

Was it the horn? She fumbled a few notes, and tried to play too fast, but her tone was exceptional, and she was so strange, so unlike any bassoonist he'd met, that he knew he wanted to take her on as a student.

Then the solo was over. Herminda stopped, held her horn up by the side of her chair like a piece of artillery, and was quiet for a moment. He could tell she'd relaxed. She looked at him as if to inquire, "Well?", but said nothing.

"What key is that in? B-flat?" Gerald asked, leaning over to take another cigarette from the bowl on the table. "Play me that scale."

She played the B-flat scale.

"Play it slower, like you did when you were warming up."

She played it again, holding each note of the scale four counts.

"Now hold that scale in your mind, each sound of it, and play the piece again." He fingered the cigarette, not intending to light it, just to hold it. She frowned at him, then closed her eyes for a moment and played the piece again. The first difficult low note was no problem, and the whole solo was smooth and graceful.

"Let me see your reed," he said.

She untwisted it, blew out the saliva, and wiped it on her sleeve in a gesture of courtesy. Gerald put out his cigarette, looked at the reed and then blew on it, making a chirpy, birdlike squeak.

"It's way too hard a reed for this piece. Where'd you get this?"

"Over at Baxter's." Her lips were tight. She wasn't going to offer him anything extra.

"You should be making your own reeds."

"Oh." Her face reddened, although he hadn't meant to embarrass her.

"How long have you been playing bassoon, Herminda?" His tongue tripped a little over her name.

Herminca sat back slightly in the chair, laying the bassoon across her lap. "I played oboe when I was in junior high, but the high school orchestra needed a bassoon." She pushed her hair off her face and glanced at him. "I haven't played real regular for a while, but I've felt like, you know, starting up again. Paul Murray—he's the conductor of the Youth Symphony—he said I should get lessons. He said I should call you."

"So you're about 20, am I correct?" Gerald handed her back her reed.

"20, yes," she nodded, eyeing the reed he had just tested with distaste.

"Are you playing with a group now?"

She hesitated, as if wondering whether her answer would affect her chances to work with him.

"No."

"Why did you start playing again, especially if you're not playing with a group?"

She looked at the floor. "Oh, I don't know. It feels like I've always played. I rented a horn."

"This one's not rented," he said, eyeing the red cherry wood with the *Fox* insignia on the curve of the bell.

"No, I bought it used a couple years ago. I got a loan from my uncle."

They were both quiet a moment. Gerald finished his cigarette, stood up, and put it out in the sink.

"Well, Mr. Poolan," she said with a hint of a sigh, "will you give me lessons?" It was both a quiet question and a defiant one, and Gerald appreciated that she didn't ask, *Am I good enough?* He didn't want to work with someone asking him that question.

He turned from the sink to face her. "I would be glad to work with you, Herminda, if you're serious about it."

"I'm serious." Her gaze was steady, the black eyes calm. Her eyes were much older than the rest of her.

"Then we need to get you playing with a group. I have another student, Richard, and he might play some duets with you. Perhaps I'll schedule him in on one of your lessons."

She shrugged.

"What did you expect to pay for lessons, Herminda?"

"I don't know," she stammered. "Maybe, like twenty-five bucks an hour?"

"Twenty-five, then." (Richard paid him fifty.)

She nodded.

"Next week, then, this time?" he said. "Go ahead and work on that exercise, and all the scales. *All* of them. I'll see if I can dig up some music."

She nodded. "Gerald—is it okay that I call you that?— I was wondering, one other thing. I wondered whether *you'd* play the exercise," Herminda said, then added in a rush, "I mean, I would like to hear someone else play it. Better."

Gerald hesitated, then put his hand out for the horn and retrieved his own reeds from the small black case in his shirt pocket. As he selected a reed, moistened it in his mouth, and twisted it onto Herminda's bassoon he realized he was pleased at her request. He played a few notes to try it out, then came in on the first note of the solo from underneath it, with no grumbling from the horn. The room filled up with the warm, woody sound. It was a good instrument.

When he was finished, he gave her back the horn. It wasn't exactly fair; he'd played this exercise many times before.

"Thank you. The Fox likes you," Herminda said, and smiled genuinely for the first time since he had opened the door. Her cool face changed immensely in that smile. She was like a very old child.

"Pardon me?"

"The Fox—I call him the Fox sometimes. He's like an animal, you know. Plays good for you when he knows you like him." She smiled again and stood up to dismantle her horn.

"Oh." Gerald didn't know what to say. He had never thought of his basscon as an animal, only as an instrument, a tool.

He almost smiled. "You're welcome. That is a nice instrument you have." The phone rang and he moved to get it. It would be John, with arrangements for dinner. Herminda packed up her horn as he answered. He covered the mouthpiece.

"You can see yourself out?"

She nodded.

"Next week, then."

Gerald had always given his neighbor downstairs warning about the noise from his students and his own practicing, but she said she didn't hear much noise and, in any case, it didn't bother her. "That bassoon has such a...*friendly* sound to it," she often said.

It was both amusing and annoying that the essence of the instrument he had played most of his life would be described as "friendly," but his neighbor was right. So much music written for the bassoon made it sound like a sort of romping dog, chasing the children, nipping their heels, guarding them.

With Herminda he now had three students, and that was more than enough. Gerald didn't consider himself a particularly good teacher; he was impatient. He got tired of rephrasing the same points over and over again, and it was hard to mask his boredom if progress was slower than he thought it should be. Other than the extra money that his students brought in, he had felt lately there was not much reason to teach. The thought made him sad in a vague sort of way. Once, after listening in on the end of a lesson with Richard, John told him that he sounded so unsupportive that if *he* were taking lessons from Gerald he'd probably burst into tears and not come back.

"You have to understand Richard," he had replied, although he supposed John was right. He was detached.

His youngest student was Sheila Ziesing, the oboist's 18-year-old daughter, and although Howard Ziesing paid well for the lessons, they both considered the arrangement a favor. Sheila wasn't talented like her father, but she practiced most of the time and seemed to enjoy the music, and who could tell? She would probably quit by the time her senior prom came around and would perhaps encourage her future children to take piano lessons.

Richard, a tall man in his early 30's, with brown hair and glasses, was the student he had had the longest, for four years. Gerald tended to think that, like himself, Richard looked like a bassoon player, not attractive or exactly unattractive. Richard had played since he was in junior high school, and now he played for the San Jose Symphony. He didn't really need lessons; Gerald didn't see what good they were doing, and he had told Richard this several times. Technically Richard was very apt, very quick. It was this technicality, though, that hurt him.

Perhaps it was something easier to describe in a pianist than a bassoonist. It was subtle, something Gerald could hear in Richard's tone, something that didn't go away. If there were a law degree in music, Richard would have gotten it long ago. He followed the directions, the intonation, crescendos and pianissimos; he controlled the horn, and finally his feeling for the instrument and for the music was mechanical. Gerald had tried to discuss this with him, and Richard pursed his lips, furrowed his brow, and nodded respectfully. He had no idea what Gerald was talking about, even though he had been playing for 20 years or so. Gerald had attempted to make this thing, the *tone*, the bottom-line approach to practice. Richard thought the lessons were improving his style. Perhaps he hoped Gerald would be a contact for him if there was ever a permanent opening in the symphony in the city. It seemed to Gerald like an expensive contact, and he was going to ask him to cut down to every other week—the most he could do for Richard, who would probably take this cheerfully as a sign that he was ready for what he called "the big leagues."

In the six months since the audition, he and Herminda had developed a routine. She never paused in his living room, but was comfortable in the large kitchen, the sun angling through the window at the same time each week. Or, when it was gray outside, the light from a brass lamp on the table pooling over the floor. After that first audition she usually wore huge, unattractive tee-shirts (usually black) tucked into baggy jeans that hung precariously on her small hips as though at any moment they might slip off, and sneakers.

"Do you ever cook in here?" she asked, once.

"Of course."

She shrugged. "It's just so...*clean*. And no smells. Except for those disgusting cigarettes."

He had occasionally offered her a cup of coffee after a lesson and when she stayed, she did most of the talking. Her mother didn't speak English, and also worked in the produce store; she had two younger sisters and an older brother; her sisters called her "Meanie" and her mother and brother called her "Minda"; she was always considered an outsider in high school, and graduated a year early (although she still came back to school for orchestra rehearsals and performances). Gerald enjoyed these conversations; her life was so curiously different from his, so full of people and bustle. He didn't know how she could practice.

"You make good coffee," she had said the other week, surprised. "Better than at the cafe."

"Well, that's hopeful." It had been a long lesson, very focused, and he felt invigorated. Herminda finally seemed to be understanding the concept of slowing down and was doing it without his prompting. There was a lull, and he felt he should say something.

"Do you like waitressing?" he asked.

She shrugged. "Yeah. I guess I do. I think I get paid what I'm worth, for once. The people, they pay you for *you*, not just your work. Unlike my uncle's place. I still owe him a lot on this bassoon—like a couple thousand dollars."

Gerald didn't like to talk about money. It might not be past her, he thought, to do a sob story and ask for a break in the lesson fees. "Oh," he said, standing to dissemble his horn.

"Does it hurt the horn to be in a cold place?" she asked as she, too, began taking her horn apart and swabbing it out.

"Only if it's *very* cold," he replied, "and you don't move it from cold to very hot. It'll crack the wood."

"Yeah, my room has no heat, and I've been wondering about that."

Where would her room be that it had no heat? he wondered. He tried to picture it and couldn't. Herminda's voice sounded very matter-of-fact. She didn't elaborate; Gerald didn't ask.

Herminda was no prodigy. At 20, she was too old, for one thing. And prodigies did not make their debut on the bassoon. Gerald knew he made her angry with his unmaskable impatience, but she played better when she was angry. She was in awe of technical competence; the exercise she had chosen for her audition was full of notes. Herminda had a soloist mentality, often pushing the sound to the point of strain, as if she must make herself *heard*, although the bassoon was rarely heard unless the rest of the orchestra was pianissimo. The horn had many ranges, but primarily it was a background instrument, watchful, not a solo instrument. And although there were bassoon solos written by most of the major composers, they were relatively few. He tried to explain this to her.

When you played enough solos, Gerald thought, you didn't crave them so much. What you began to desire was the perfection of the whole piece, and so you depended on everyone. The dependence was tiresome; there was a lot of back-biting, and Gerald had done his share. For instance, Sheila Ziesing's father, the first oboist—such a greasy, homophobic man with those gray polyester suits and thick, smug lips—but when they were coming to Section K, Howard would give him a little nod and suddenly they were *playing* together. Basically, Gerald disliked Howard, but Howard was a good musician, and they had this intimacy, as he had with the rest of the orchestra. It was like a giant family. You didn't choose them; you were stuck with them; you depended on them to play well until they left, or retired, or were fired. And they depended on you.

He'd told his friend Stephen about Herminda soon after that first encounter, in April. Stephen Greenberg, Gerald's oldest friend in the city, worked in the Symphony box office, and he loved hearing about Gerald's students. There had been quite a number of them over the years. A few had found positions; most went on to other lives.

He was intrigued by Gerald's description. "And she's just been playing alone? Like it's a guitar? Like, whip-out-the-horn-let's-play-a-few-numbers?"

Gerald shrugged.

"Strange."

Gerald agreed. Without a group to play with, he wasn't sure what Herminda intended to do with the lessons. Improvement for improvement's sake? He didn't want her to be disappointed. No, more, *he* didn't want to be disappointed. In the past months he'd heard her improve, and the best thing right now would be to get her playing *with* someone. Gerald had invited Richard over a couple of times so that Herminda could work on duets with someone else, but he knew she didn't like him. He'd been surprised at Richard's condescension when he first met Herminda, his amused glance at Gerald to see if he was serious. Perhaps that was how Gerald himself had been when he first met her, he thought. Richard's attitude changed when he heard Herminda play, but Gerald decided not to bring them together again.

He'd heard through the grapevine that Berkowski was going to do *Rite of Spring* for next May, and with Cynthia Houseworth pregnant he was going to need a good second bassoon. Gerald had it in mind as he watched Herminda go through the lessons.

But she had to do something else, first. He talked to Ralph Gertz, first clarinetist, about a musical he'd volunteered to conduct *Man of La Mancha* over in Berkeley. Gertz said no other bassoonists had auditioned so if she wanted the part and could play even half-decently Herminda had the part. There was no money, just work.

"*Man of La Mancha!* Gerald? Oh, *c'mon,*" Herminda exclaimed with disdain when he told her, muttering something else in Spanish that he didn't understand. He understood her reluctance, but he shrugged and acted miffed. This was the way it was between them; she got cocky, and she looked to Gerald to stare her down, and so he did. Herminda was quiet and rigorous, and there was something in her, some drive, that made Gerald feel hopeful for her. Maybe she could even get a position if she went back to school. As a Latina, they'd be clamoring for her. He didn't know. It could also hold her up or make her quit. It was too early to be talking about these things. He knew how much work it was. Sometimes that was all he knew.

Chapter 2

Herminda watched the couple at the table in the far corner of her section. A huge Eye-of-God made from red, gold, and white polyester yarn hung on the wall over their table and looked like it was watching them, too. The woman had her shoe off—actually, it was a boot, a huge black work boot—and was stroking the man's leg (he was wearing black jeans) with her black-tight-covered foot. Up, stroke-stroke, then down. Who would have thought such a gentle foot resided in such ugly boots? Both of them were dressed entirely in black, and had ordered black bean soup and corn bread, and dark Bass Ale. There was an old shelf with some used books of little value to anyone precariously mounted on the wall over the man's head, designed to give the corner a cozy, cafe kind of feeling. That seat always made Herminda nervous. One day the books would fall; perhaps someone would get hurt; there would be a mess of black bean soup or vegetarian lasagna, and she would lose a tip.

It was mid-afternoon, and the couple was the only table she had, and she wished they would get on with it, and get home to bed, if that's where they were going. Herminda went over to the counter by the huge bulletin board listing apartment vacancies, used musical instruments and cars for sale, missing animals, poems, a few personal ads, and probably 30 flyers for all kinds of events in the city. From across the huge cavern of the cafe, the bulletin board looked like a badly-made paper quilt. She washed the counter and straightened the stools under it. She liked the disorder of the café, such a contrast to her uncle's produce shop, even though she didn't like how dark the cafe always was. cafe *Del Sol.* It should have been cafe *del las Sombras,* and cut it with the so-called Latin flavor, she thought. There wasn't one ethnic dish on the menu.

At her uncle's produce shop, just down four blocks from the cafe on the corner of 21st and Mission Streets, every pear and pepper had its place in a bin, and her uncle still yelled at her, even after four years working there, if something wasn't just so. Like a painter, he would squint for an overall effect as he left her in charge the two evenings a week that she worked and could always spot a jalapeno in with the bells.

"Minda, *compraron mas cuando sea perfecto, cuando tenga orden,*" he'd say. People buy more when it's perfect, when it has order.

"*Escuche a tu tío, Minda,*" her mother would pitch in. Listen to your uncle, Minda.

Working with them made her feel like she was still 11 most of the time. If she could get more hours at the café she could quit the fucking job.

Fucking, she thought to herself, thinking of the way her girlfriends in high school could make the word sound like some kind of dangerous machine in a factory that could flatten you with one huge stomp: FUCKin, FUCKin, FUCKin. She'd practiced it, using it as an adjective, but it didn't suit her. Over at Clarice's house (before Clarice had gotten hooked up with Stefan), she and Clarice used to mimic the other girls. The word sounded ridiculous, coming from her small body. Ridiculous in the same way those gigantic tin earrings her girlfriends wore, sometimes lined up on their lobes five and six together.

"Ridiculous," she said under her breath. She preferred two small diamond studs.

Herminda glanced over at the couple. She could only see the man's face from this angle, and she could tell beneath his friendly, sensitive look he was thinking about fucking. And so was the girl, her foot still on his leg, not embarrassed about Herminda seeing it all. She shrugged; why should she care? Why should any of this bother her so much? She had her music. She was going to be a musician; she was going to make it, and it was going to take all her attention.

"Minda," a man's voice sang quietly from the kitchen. "*¿Qué tal, chiquita?*" Mickey said. She had taught him to say that. Mickey was the cafe's manager-slash-part-time cook, as he described himself, and was there most of the hours she was. He had hired her just before the summer, and she had come to like him. He was efficient, never rude like the other cook, and there was always an affection in his voice that didn't sound to her like *fucking.* He was about 30; thin and wiry, with thick red hair the color of Gerald's (although unlike Gerald he had a lot of hair), and that white, freckled skin that went with it. Sometimes he wore glasses. He made the vegetarian lasagna and the peach cobbler and trained everyone how to run the espresso machine. He was divorced and had a son who lived with him. Sometimes he talked to Herminda about his son, Christopher, about picking him up from daycare, and what was he going to do when it came time for kindergarten—the public schools in the city being so bad, and the private schools being so expensive and hard to get into.

Except for the freckled skin, she thought Mickey was almost attractive. She didn't know if she thought this in some objective way, or if she'd become attracted since she'd noticed a slight

change in his voice when he spoke to her the past few weeks—
that singing sound that let her know he was interested in her. He
was probably going to ask her out, and she was trying to decide
if she'd go.

If he asked she'd say Yes. He was a nice guy, an older man,
not like those *sinverguenzas* she'd hoped to know in high school
and (lucky for her) didn't get. Mickey was easy to talk to. Maybe
he'd take her out to dinner, for a drink, back to his place? Her
throat tightened; did she want to go back to his place? What
would his place be like? She watched his strong, freckled hands
chopping up eggplant from over the order-up counter—quick
and white, his hands, almost like Gerald's. But Gerald's hands
were shorter, and thinner. And he was a queer.

"So how's it going?" Mickey said. "Slow today, huh?"

"Yeah. I think that couple is going to slip under their table
any second now," she said with a tilt of her head toward the
corner table. Mickey glanced over at them; his eyebrows went up
and down in a joking way and he smiled.

"So, Herminda, how're the music lessons going?"

"Good. I've got a lesson when I get off," she said, "and then
he's got me hooked up to play in the orchestra for a musical in
Berkeley. In a couple of months."

"No kidding. What's the musical?" Mickey scooped up the
chopped eggplant with both hands and let it drop into a huge
steaming kettle on the restaurant stove.

"Don't laugh."

"I won't."

"*Man of La Mancha.*"

"*To DREAM, the impossible DREAM....*" Mickey began to
sing.

Herminda blushed. "Yeah, yeah, yeah. You said you wouldn't laugh."

"I couldn't control myself. But that's great. It's something, anyway. Better than busting your balls making vegetarian lasagna forty hours a week." Mickey's voice was cheerful and resigned. He wiped his hands on a white towel that was tucked into the front of his jeans.

"So, Herminda," he said, casually, stirring the kettle, and she knew it was coming, and held the corners of her mouth tight to keep from smiling, "I've been meaning to ask you for a couple weeks. But then, I don't know. I mean, I don't know if you're seeing anyone. But even if you are, we could still just go, as friends, you know."

"You trying to say something, Mick?"

He smiled and looked at her. "Yeah. You want to go out? The movie I meant to ask you to is already gone, but we could go somewhere else, get some dinner, or something."

"Sure. Okay. When?"

"Friday?"

"I have to work the produce shop Friday night. Saturday?"

"Saturday. You're working in the afternoon here, right? I'll just come by and get you when you get off."

"Okay." She didn't want to sound too enthusiastic; she didn't want him to think she was too eager, that she'd only been on two dates in her life, both boring disasters, and that other time that didn't count.

The bell over the cafe door tinkled. "You got a customer," Mickey said, and went back to his cooking.

Herminda smiled mechanically, squinting slightly to make out the dark figure in the doorway. A young man, in his early twenties. He chose a table by the window, put his duffel bag down beside him, and looked around.

"Hi," Herminda said, handing him a menu, thinking he *would* choose the farthest table from the kitchen.

"Hi," the man said, slipping off his denim jacket. "I just want a cappuccino. Whole milk, please." He was a couple years older than her, 22 or 23, with blonde hair and tanned, acne-scarred skin. Queer, she judged, from the well-cared-for hands, and khaki slacks and a collared white tee-shirt.

Herminda took the menu back and went behind the counter to make the cappuccino. It wasn't that she hated queers, like her brother did. "Jesus Christ, Minda, they fuck each other in the ass!" he'd said. "It's disgusting! It's against the Church."

She had thought that being against the Church was a pretty lame excuse for hating queers, since her family hadn't gone to Mass since their mother stopped forcing them several years ago. If guys wanted to do it to each other, it was fine with her. Most of the time she was grateful to be ignored. She hadn't really known that many gays. Gerald was the first homosexual she'd actually had anything to do with, and he was a decent person. She'd known mostly by his place, the way it was all done in white and everything so perfect, unlike any men she'd ever known. It had made her nervous. But she'd taken lessons now for six months and she trusted Gerald and respected his talent.

It was just the way they acted like they owned the world sometimes. At least this world, here in the city. Her brother was right about that, anyway. They had money. She envied them their money.

She took the man his cappuccino.

"Thanks," he said, and smiled at her. His eyes were bright blue.

The other table was ready to leave, and she gave them their check. It was almost the end of her shift, and when she remembered the man by the window he had already finished his coffee and left. There were three dollars on the table, a fifty-percent tip. They usually did leave good tips, she thought, even when they were ignoring you. It would go with the rest of the tip money into an envelope to pay for her bassoon lesson this week.

Herminda had bought herself a small men's jacket, black wool, for the winter, and with her black hair and dark glasses she liked the way she looked in the store windows. She looked cool, non-categorical, the battered bassoon case on the tote behind her like some kind of modern bag lady. (She had gotten a second, beat-up bassoon case to lessen the likelihood of theft.) She always caught jeers and questions from the guys hanging out in Dolores Park, so usually she walked the sidewalks around the perimeter.

It wasn't a bad walk to Gerald's place on Hill Street, except in the rain. The walk gave her time to think, to visualize the lesson ahead and think of the music. It was a meditation, thinking of the music, and she loved the way just imagining the sound of her horn would take her away from herself. She pictured the material she had worked on during the week, and the way the notes looked on the page, and the way the first few bars sounded. From those cues she could usually go through much of the score for the lesson. It was like a photographic hearing. If she had gone through the exercise or piece a few times, and memorized the way it opened on the page, it inhabited her. It was easy to recall the sections that were difficult and go over them in her mind. When Gerald had asked her how she practiced, she'd told him how she would think about the music and he had just looked at her strangely. He hadn't said, *Don't do that.*

Today, however, Herminda wasn't thinking about the lesson; she was thinking about Mickey, and about going out Saturday night, and what she would wear. She didn't want to think too much about it, but she couldn't help it. It was a different kind of meditation, and she forgot what she was doing and walked through Dolores Park instead of around it. A crowd of kids, 13- and 14-year-olds, stood under the palm trees drinking beer. From the corner of her eye she recognized one of them, Tomas, a friend of her younger sister's. These kids were probably all in gangs, or waiting to be allowed in. In a few years, if nothing happened to them, they'd be like Ricardo.

Her brother was three years older than her, and he hung out here in the park at night, when he could get away with it. He fixed cars with one of his cousins, Raul, and had recently moved in with him. He drank a lot, but so far he wasn't into drugs, and he wasn't in a gang. Herminda loved Ricardo. He was gentle with her, and with her sisters. He avoided their mother, but left them money, and kidded around with her and her sisters when he was at the house. She didn't like to think of him living with Raul, who was like his brother Felix. It wasn't going to be good. She could feel it. And the cops were out more these days, looking for guys like her brother.

"Hey, *chiquita*, what you got in your big purse?" the boys jeered. "What's in your big BOX?" They laughed, and she pushed on fiercely up the sidewalk, ignoring them, and they were not interested enough to pursue her. Sometimes she wished the bassoon was like an umbrella, something she could flick a button and out it would pop, fully assembled. All she'd have to do would be to point it at them and watch their balls shrivel up.

Herminda was sweating from the trek up the hill. At the top of Church Street she came out of the afternoon shadows into sun and turned around as she usually did to look at the view. It was a clear fall afternoon, with no haze over the East Bay. Everything looked bright and airy, and beige. She imagined the tall, dark brick buildings of New York, where her mother had grown up, and they had lived until she was two. Someone in the park started up some music at highest volume, some rap song. But it sounded happy and at this peak, on the broad, white sidewalk, she felt safe. As she turned onto Hill Street, Herminda thought of the small, ivy-outlined entrance to Gerald's place, and the way his flat smelled of books, and sometimes of coffee. It seemed far from the real world, and she was comfortable there.

Sometimes half a lesson was just scales, tone, breath control. It drove her crazy at first, but she had gotten used to it. Gerald told her every piece she played would be easier if she was confident with these basics. Occasionally they played together—either the same piece, in unison, or from a book of duets he had. This was what she liked, playing together. Herminda wanted to take the duets book home and work on them, but it was his sight-reading work for her. "Anticipate," he said when they did the sight-reading. "Look it over like you were skimming a book; hear the notes in your head before you ever put the horn to your mouth."

I do that all the time, she thought. I'm always sight-reading.

Sometimes Gerald would offer her a cup of coffee after a lesson, and they would talk for about ten minutes before conversation became awkward. She was prompt after every lesson to pack up her horn and get ready to leave at a regular pace so he wouldn't think she was stalling for an invitation. Gerald enjoyed these conversations, too, she thought, even though she did most of the talking. Each time that she resolved she would talk less, and ask *him* something, she was flattered by his attention and found herself going on. Last week he'd asked her what her father did for a living.

"Oh, he's gone a long time. Since Silvia—my sister—was a baby," she explained, swabbing out the mid-section of her bassoon. "He took off. Too much for him," she attempted a laugh. "He met my mother when she was visiting New York from Chile. He was white, you know," she added, as if that explained his leaving. Gerald examined her, a look of curiosity on his face, and she felt herself flush.

"*My* father took off without going anywhere," he said.

"What do you mean?" Gerald rarely said anything personal to her.

"He would arrive home from work—30 years at the same place —ask me if I'd done my homework, heat up two delicious TV dinners and watch television until time to 'hit the sack'. 'Guess I'll hit the sack,' he'd say. That's the way it was for 10 years until I got out of there."

"But what about your mother?"

"She died when I was 11."

"Oh, well, that's why he was that way."

"That was no excuse. The grief wasn't all his," Gerald said briskly, and Herminda could tell the conversation was at an end. She hoped he wasn't angry at her. She closed her case.

Gerald walked her to the door. "It was a good lesson," he said decisively. "I'm pleased with the improvement." Now he was embarrassed; she could tell by the stiff way he spoke. From behind her sunglasses she could look at Gerald more closely, his pale freckled skin and three deep wrinkles across his forehead. She tried to imagine his boyfriend kissing that forehead, but couldn't.

"I'll see you next week. I'll have that *Man of La Mancha* music by then," he said, with a brief smile, and closed the door behind her.

Chapter 3

Two weeks before Thanksgiving, an unusually warm front hung over the city for three days, almost like spring. "C'mon," Stephen said, rummaging in Gerald's refrigerator. "We've got to go to the park. It's too beautiful out."

"And what are we going to do there—play frisbee?" Gerald protested half-heartedly. He had just finished a lesson with Herminda and all he wanted to do was take a nap out on the deck.

"You should be so agile," Stephen replied, now searching through the cabinets. "Ah. I can count on you to have at least one decent bottle of wine in your cupboard, Miss Hubbard." He pulled a bottle of Beaujolais from the wine rack, took a couple of wine glasses from a different cupboard, wrapped them in a dishtowel and put everything into his backpack.

"We're set. I suppose you don't want to change," he said, giving Gerald's slacks and button-down shirt a sour look.

"Change into what? Bathing trunks?"

Stephen laughed, a big laugh with his head thrown back, and Gerald loved to hear it. Stephen went into the bathroom and came out with two large towels. "No, I guess you're fine. We wouldn't want you to be more, or less, than you are, Ger."

Before they left, Gerald called John and invited him to meet them at the park. During the pause on the phone, Gerald imagined John looking at his watch, calculating whether it was an appropriate time to end his working day.

"I might join you if you're still there in half an hour. And then where would you like to go for dinner tonight?" Another pause. "We can invite Stephen." John didn't understand Stephen's humor or his under-employment. Since Stephen's diagnosis, however, John had tried to lighten up and went out of his way to include him.

"I don't know," Gerald said. "Perhaps we could go to the Thai place at the end of 24th."

"Sounds good. See you at the park."

Despite Gerald's protests, they walked. Stephen held onto Gerald's arm at the steepest part of the hill, and then they turned onto Church Street. At Dolores Park, they stationed themselves at Stephen's favorite spot on the still-sunny terrace of grass where they could survey the playground and the tennis courts at the other end. Stephen took off his shirt to reveal a wilted purple tee-shirt that read in yellow script: *Symphonic Sycophant*. "See," he'd said once, "you could change the *h* in Sycophant and make it an *l* and it'd be Symphonic Psycho-Plant, which I also like. I might make one of those." Stephen had a friend at a silk-screening shop who would make tee-shirts for him at cost if he ordered as least ten. He never used illustrations, only slogans. Sometimes the sayings were funny, sometimes they were stupid, sometimes they were merely unintelligible. Gerald also had one of the Sycophant shirts, but his was clean, never worn, in a large plastic clothes storage box in the closet.

Stephen uncorked the wine, poured it, and put the bottle back discreetly into the paper bag. "Cheers," he said, and they drank. He grabbed Gerald's hand and pressed it to the back of his neck.

"Feel that, warm? That's how a body should feel. Yes." He leaned back on the beach towel, the back of his head resting on one hand. The inside of his upper arm was white and smooth, like a boy's, a blue vein running just below the surface in an extended *S*.

Gerald remembered when Stephen was first diagnosed last year. He had come over to the house as he often did on summer afternoons when he didn't have to work. "I'm positive," he blurted out at the front door, so quickly that Gerald was waiting for the rest of the sentence: "I'm positive *of...* I'm positive *that...*" He hadn't known that Stephen was going for the test. And then Stephen began to cry and fell into Gerald's arms. He spent most of the afternoon with Gerald on the couch, in waves of hysteria. Gerald envied Stephen's naturalness, the way his terror and anger and helplessness all came out unedited, unrefined. Neither of them knew what the diagnosis meant in Stephen's particular case except, most likely, dying. But dying could happen many different ways, in many time frames. They'd both seen that.

"*Díme! Díme!*" A small boy screamed at his mother in the playground. *Give me.*

It *was* a magnificent day, and each of the downtown buildings seemed cut out and grafted back onto the cloudless blue sky. A few mothers and children milled about in the playground and a young couple hung on each other as they made their way along the diagonal sidewalk through the park. Quiet, even for a weekday afternoon. In the old days, on a warm day like today, the grassy terrace would be lined with sunbathing men, mostly night workers, bartenders and waiters, Stephen among them on his days off, Gerald only occasionally (and only with Stephen)— but now it was empty.

They didn't talk. Impossible to tell whether Stephen's eyes were open or shut beneath the dark mirrored glasses.

The exercise Herminda had played for him on her bassoon that morning (and he for her) went on in Gerald's head. It started low and rambled up into the high range, then quickly back and forth, testing the embouchure. It was a good melody as well as a good exercise, and he was glad he'd chosen it. He thought of her thin fingers over the holes, really quite something. He wondered if Herminda crossed through the park to get to his house.

"When's your *boyfriend* arriving?" Stephen teased Gerald.

"Soon, I hope. There's still a glass of wine left."

Stephen laid back down on his towel, even though they were in shadow now.

"Are you having trouble with John?" Gerald asked.

"Trouble with John, the love of your life?" Stephen's arm was draped across his eyes, so Gerald couldn't see what his real mood was. "No, I don't have trouble with him. But he needn't be so *nice*, you know?"

John arrived within 15 minutes, as he said he would, and Gerald laid his towel horizontally so John could sit without staining his suit. As sloppy as he was at his own apartment, John was pristine about his suits. Stephen poured him the last of the wine, saving a sip for Gerald and himself.

"We three queens of orient are," he sang, buoyantly, his hand held out toward the horizon in a toast, "Bearing gifts we travel afar. Field and fountain, moor and mou-ountain, following yonder star."

Stephen laughed, and John rolled his eyes. "What's he *on?*" John asked Gerald playfully.

"Actually, these days I'm on a steady diet of AZT and Bactrim, and ten or twenty other vitamins on the Vitamina Vegamin Regimen," Stephen quipped, irritated.

"Geez, Stephen!"

"*Boys*," Gerald reprimanded.

A spray of liquid came down over Stephen, splashing Gerald's left arm. There was laughing from the sidewalk above, and by the time Gerald discerned that some kids had opened a compressed can of beer over them, Stephen had jumped up and was chasing them. There were two boys and a girl, maybe 14 or 15 years old. Gerald and John both clambered up to the sidewalk. Gerald wanted to call out to Stephen to stop—who could tell if the kids carried a gun?—but didn't. He didn't want them to know Stephen's name.

Stephen chased them almost out of the park, surprisingly quick on his feet, and then one of the kids tossed another beer can over his shoulder. It exploded on the sidewalk and Stephen jumped out of the way. They disappeared into the open streetcar tunnel, and Stephen slowed down and stopped, his hands on his hips. Was he swearing? From this distance Stephen looked like he was only about 18 himself. After a moment, he turned and walked back slowly toward them.

John was wiping Gerald's arm off with the beach towel. "Nothing like a pleasant afternoon at the park," John muttered under his breath. He was thinking Stephen had provoked the razing with his singing. Gerald took the towel and tossed it to Stephen as he came toward them. Up close, Stephen was pale and sweating, livid.

"I think I've had enough for one day," Stephen said, drying himself, heading down toward where they had been sitting for his jacket.

"Let's get a cab," John said. "We'll drop you off."

"A cab? As you may remember, I live just around the corner. I'll walk," Stephen retorted, putting on his jacket over the beer-stained tee-shirt. Now his face was pink.

John shrugged helplessly at Gerald.

Gerald kissed Stephen on the cheek and told him he would pick him up the next day, the regular time. "I'm okay," Stephen said over his shoulder as he walked off.

John started to say something as they watched him leave, then stopped. Gerald suddenly wasn't feeling too well himself— perhaps it was the wine—and he begged off dinner. John walked him back to the house, protesting all the way that if he wasn't feeling well they could call a cab. At the door, John hesitated.

"It's one of those evenings, isn't it," he said, meaning Gerald would prefer to be alone. Gerald nodded. At one point they had considered living together, but Gerald didn't think he could live with anyone. Except for those years with his father after his mother died, he had always lived alone. It was his way. He unlocked the door, then turned and put his hand on John's arm.

John looked down at his arm and smiled weakly. "I don't like these evenings, you know," he said.

"I know." All he would have to do is say, *Oh, come in.* They would settle in around each other and the evening would be fine. "Let's go out tomorrow," he said.

"I'm in LA tomorrow. A one-o'clock flight."

"I'd forgotten."

John looked at his watch, which is what he did when he'd run out of things to say. He leaned over and kissed Gerald lightly. "Look, why don't *you* call *me*. Friday. I'll be back then."

Now John was irritated *and* hurt; this one would take some smoothing over. Gerald disliked himself for thinking this way, as though he were the narrator and not the...lover. They were lovers, weren't they? He and John? He could still say, *Oh, come in.*

And then the moment was gone, and John was down the steps with a wave that was meant to be casual but was stiff, almost admonishing. Gerald watched him hike up the street, purposefully, his dark suit jacket flapping out at either side until he reached around and buttoned them shut as he rounded the corner out of sight.

Stephen hated the traffic jams on 24th Street, so Gerald always drove him to his bi-monthly appointments at the hospital on the back streets of the Mission. Stephen didn't like Potrero Avenue either, so Gerald turned onto Florida. Herminda lived on this street—either this one or Bryant, he couldn't remember. The stuccoed houses were all so close to the street, which was rough and spattered with potholes. The hot spell was over; the day had started off chilly and clear, more like the way a November day should be.

"I guess it's time," Stephen said with a sigh.

"Time for what?" Sometimes he didn't care for Stephen's grand pronouncements. They'd seen more of each other in the past six months than in the previous six years, and he'd heard a lot of pronouncements.

"Time to do *Rite of Spring* again. Weren't we just talking about it?" Stephen pulled his jacket around him tighter. He was definitely in a pissy mood. Gerald was sure he was thinking about the incident at the park yesterday, but neither of them had brought it up.

Gerald had told him about the program Berkowski had cooked for May: Stravinsky's *Rite of Spring*, Ravel's *Bolero*, and one of the Rossini overtures. Since he'd been diagnosed, Stephen had gone part-time in the Box Office, but he still took every program decision as a personal affront or affirmation. *Rite* was his favorite piece of music. "It's urban," Stephen used to say. "It's mean, and cold, and amazing. It predicts... everything." He'd meant the rest of the long 20th century—the Revolution, and the world wars.

"But *Bolero*?" Stephen continued. "Christ, give me a break. Is the fourth grade of SF Public Schools doing a field trip to Davies Hall or something?" He was agitated.

Gerald reached over and squeezed his arm. "Stephen," he said, and they were both quiet.

Stephen had been one of a few to get into an experimental program at San Francisco General, but had had a violent reaction to the first medication they tried and after that decided to go to regular treatment of AZT and Bactrim, which he handled much better. Stephen had been careful. He hadn't gotten very, very sick. Only one hospitalization in 18 months (it was funny how they talked about the disease in terms of months, like a baby's age: 10 months, 12 months, 18 months...), and that was at the beginning, when he responded badly to the drugs. Some days he was hopeful; he thought he would live a long time. Other days not. Gerald rode on the tails of Stephen's moods. He was far too cynical himself to tell Stephen he might get better, or might not. Stephen was still himself. He hadn't become a burden.

He'd lost about 20 pounds with the new treatment, and he was looking almost handsome in a wan sort of way. His brown hair had a grayish tone to it now, like metal—or maybe it was the gray jacket he was wearing. With his hair combed back, his forehead practically gleamed.

"Stop looking at me, Gerald," he said, although Gerald knew that, in a way, Stephen liked him to look. A couple of weeks before as Gerald drove him home Stephen had said, "You know, it's almost sexual, this dying." He'd been about to go into one of his spiels, probably, one of his analyses about how having AIDS gave him all kinds of bodily attention he'd rarely had when he was well, but Gerald had begun to cry and he'd stopped. He and Stephen had never been lovers, but he hated how he knew what Stephen meant, how their focus had gone more and more toward the body and how it could change. How strange and beautiful it could be, and how dangerous. Some days he looked ghostly, some days handsome, like today, and much of the time he looked like his old self—tall and ponderous and like he needed exercise.

After the first few visits they knew better than to enter through the Emergency Room at San Francisco General and made a routine of parking on Potrero Avenue, missing most of the bustle of hospital traffic, and coming in through the main door, which was dark and quiet and more sane.

They checked in and sat down among the nine or ten other people waiting to be seen, most of whom looked up briefly when Stephen and Gerald came in, and then looked down again to their reading, or their laps, or the wall decorated with cheerful, efficiently-framed pastels of lily pads and irises. It was impossible to tell how quickly Stephen would be called in —some days were fast, others were excruciating, so they both settled in wordlessly, as if for a commute. Gerald knew Stephen didn't like to talk while they were in the waiting room, but he had forgotten to bring anything to read. Still, he refused Stephen's offering of a magazine.

Nobody talked. It was a solemn place. Of the group, only a couple of people were obviously sick—a young woman with sores on her lip and on the backs of her hands, and a man who had no marks, but was impossibly thin and gray-skinned, resting with his eyes closed and his head against the wall. A couple of sullen-looking Hispanic men came in after Gerald and Stephen, one of whom stood rather than sit next to Stephen in the only seat left. Stephen never even looked in their direction, but next to him Gerald could feel his tension.

It was a quick day. The patients cleared out one by one, and finally a thin Hispanic nurse called Stephen's name. Gerald thought of Herminda, older.

"Do you want me to come in with you?" he asked.

"Not today," Stephen said.

And so Gerald sat for 45 minutes in the waiting room. He supposed he could have gone for a cup of coffee, but he never knew how long the appointment could last. Sometimes he used the waiting time as practice in being where he was, in this white room, waiting. It occurred to him that the only times in his life he wasn't planning ahead, or looking behind—the only times he was just where he was—were when he was playing bassoon (and one could easily argue that he was of course planning ahead, reading the music, anticipating the next notes), and when he was having sex. It seemed important that one should just be where one was, but he felt a kind of surrender in it that he didn't like, and an effort that seemed unnatural. There was the body, and the mind, and the other mind—was it mind?—that watched both the body and the mind.

The pastels on the wall reminded him of a set his mother did that had hung in his father's kitchen getting dusty for at least 20 years. There was an iris, he recalled, a vase of roses, and some other flower—daisies. He remembered scrutinizing the pictures on a visit home from the conservatory, as if seeing them for the first time, and thinking they weren't particularly good. He was sitting the kitchen with his father, waiting for a phone call. He must've been about 20. Gerald tuned out as his father went on about something, and then out of nowhere his father said, "I always wanted to be a singer. I always did."

"Really, Dad. I never heard that one before."

"That's why I've always been glad you've taken up music, although I don't know where it'll get you...." he eyed his son across the kitchen table. "I always had a good voice. Father Jeffries at St. Michael's said I had a career ahead of me if I put my mind to it. But I was in my mid-30's by then, and I had you and your mother to support." His father had shrugged. Gerald remembered looking closely at him, a physical image of what he himself was to become, with his slight body and prematurely bald head, once covered with red hair. His father stared out the window with his hands around the mug of coffee, the way he did much of the time since his wife had died. It was impossible for Gerald to imagine him as a singer.

"So nothing happened?"

"Oh, I took lessons. A man over in Cambridge. Figured if I was *really* good... I'd heard this guy was good. Then, on the second lesson, the guys comes around the piano and grabs me by the balls." His father made a cupping gesture. "He was a fairy, you know. I slapped that man right across the face. And then he started to cry. Bawled like a baby. Christ, just like a woman." Gerald had blushed, picking at the seam of his jeans while his gaze remained focused on the petal of a yellow daisy on the wall pastel. Then he let himself look at his father, who was shaking his head pathetically at his reminiscence, and suddenly Gerald felt free of his father, of explaining anything to him, making him understand anything. Then the phone rang —the cellist—and he had jumped to get it. That relationship hadn't lasted long. But he knew that there were at least a few others out there like himself, and he began to work harder than ever on his music.

Gerald shifted in the plastic waiting room seat. What had happened to those pastels? Jeanette was the one who had gone through his father's things after the funeral, since Gerald had had to get back for a performance, and later she shipped him the few items she thought he would want. But those pastels weren't among them. He hadn't thought of that until today. He would've liked to have them, something of his mother's.

He remembered his mother only vaguely, a slight, distant woman with bobbed brown hair. "Gerry," she always called him. He didn't like that name, just as he didn't particularly like "Gerald," but it was better than "Gerry." She died of breast cancer. In retrospect, that dying seemed quick—a few trips to the hospital, in waiting rooms like this but duller, colder. He had distanced himself, contained himself from her before she ever became sick. He did not know why. Perhaps somehow he knew she would leave. She never knew of his interest in music, or that he became a musician.

Gerald sighed and closed his eyes. He pictured himself this evening in his tux, going down the back hallway at Davies from the instrument room to the stage, his bassoon held tensely at his side, the bocal tucked in his pocket like a long-handled pipe so as not to catch on anything and get bent. His hand patting his pocket for the box of reeds. The silhouettes of Leonard and Cynthia ahead of him with their horns, like flag bearers. He imagined the expression on his face from the outside—when had he last tried to look at himself from the outside? It seemed a strange, childish thing. A posing. But still he tried to picture himself as his mother would have seen him, coming down the dimly-lit hallway with the others as he had so many times, their voices hushed, past the doors of the practice rooms, the slowly growing anticipation of performing—yes, still anticipation, thank god—the weight and murmur of the audience in the darkness, finding his seat next to Leonard and Cynthia, familiar, the music spread, perspiring slightly in the lights. An excitement. Then Berkowski, striding across stage as only he could; applause; then the *click-click* on the stand...

A young woman with a baby came into the waiting room. The nurse came out right away, cooing and exclaiming over the baby, and the two women chattered in Spanish. Gerald suspected the woman with the baby was the nurse's sister, but then the nurse was called away, and the young woman sat down in the waiting room perpendicular to him. They were the only two in the room. She smiled hesitantly at him, and he smiled back and pretended to be occupied with the magazine Stephen had left him. She couldn't be more than 19, he thought. Why was she here? Was she sick? The baby? He glanced at her covertly. Maybe she *was* the nurse's sister, but then, no, the nurse called out to her, smiling, and the woman and her baby went down the corridor to their examining room.

If they had AIDS they'd be dead, both of them, in a few years, he thought. And Stephen, too, while Gerald lived on. He felt suddenly bereft. The unfairness, all these people leaving. Stephen leaving.... His mother had never seen him perform, and now that he thought of it, neither had his father. His father died of a heart attack when he was 52—Gerald's age next year. He had never come to the Conservatory for a concert, and then he was dead.

And now suddenly there was Stephen coming down the corridor, breaking Gerald's thoughts. "My count is up! I'm in good shape!" he exclaimed, his cheeks flushed, not caring who heard. (There were only a couple of patients waiting now, both of whom tried to smile at the news, both of whom probably thought Gerald was his lover.) Stephen flung his arms around him.

Stephen insisted on taking Gerald to lunch at the Zuni Cafe, on Market Street.

"Listen," Stephen said, twirling his glass of wine, "I've been meaning to tell you. I can't make it to Thanksgiving with you and John. I want to do the soup kitchen thing in the morning—I told you about that—but then Alberto—he's in my group—asked me if I could come up and have dinner with the two of them—and he doesn't have long and I think I'll go up there. He's in Sausalito. So I hope you and John won't be all irritated about this," he finished in a rush.

He noticed that it was not an invitation. "That's okay," Gerald said, trying not to sound disappointed. Stephen had a whole new group of friends now that Gerald didn't know. It would be the first time they hadn't had Thanksgiving together, perhaps in the whole twenty years they'd known each other.

"So here's to a Thanksgiving lunch," Stephen said, toasting. He seemed relieved to have told Gerald about his plans.

He touched his glass of water to Stephen's. What would the dinner be like without Stephen? Would he and John go out? Would they cook? The questions bumbled around in the back of his head, detached, like something he had to take care of. His anxiety faded as he listened to Stephen talk about how his friend Alberto was an excellent cook and made *pollo con* something or other, with a cream sauce, and how the restaurant had changed— the bread wasn't terribly fresh, didn't he think?—and he thought he needed a firmer mattress and would Gerald help him choose one. When the food came, he watched Stephen finish a large bowl of corn chowder followed by a grilled chicken breast on rice.

"You're a cheap date," Stephen said, nodding toward Gerald's salad and cup of coffee.

Gerald just smiled. Stephen's chit-chat had soothed him somehow.

"You know," Stephen said later as Gerald dropped him off, "you really should get your new girl to play *Rite* with you." Gerald had told him about his plans for Herminda, and Stephen's comment reminded him that he had to talk to Gertz about getting the score for the musical. Since John was out of town, Gerald had offered Herminda his ticket for the performance tonight. She had accepted the ticket with a thank-you but hadn't said whether she would come.

"New blood; you need new blood," Stephen said, then smirked at his own joke. "Don't we all. I'll see you tonight."

Gerald prepared more carefully than usual that night, shaving for the second time that week and pressing his tux even though the wrinkles were hardly noticeable. The flat had a strange bright quietness tonight without John's bustling. Right now, John would be ironing the suit and having a little snack and debating whether they should get gas on the way. He hadn't called from wherever he was—Los Angeles?—and Gerald felt it almost as a reprieve. He shouldn't feel this way. He just wanted the quiet. He wanted to watch himself. The whole day had had this odd quality, a feeling of watchfulness. At the last minute he decided to take a cab rather than driving the Honda and hoping the back lot wouldn't be filled with illegally parked cars. He left all the lights on in the flat, wanting that brightness when he returned.

An hour later he was walking down the hallway with the others, just as he had pictured while in the waiting room. He imagined his mother as she would be if she were alive today, elderly, in a navy wool suit, perhaps, sitting with his father, trying to encourage him to relax and *enjoy the show...* Or, more likely, alone and comfortable alone, used to these performances, maybe even familiar with the program. She'd be listening to the conversations around her, but would remain self-contained, uncompelled to talk to anyone sitting near her.

This was, of course, ridiculous. If his mother were alive she'd be 88, and would probably be unable to stay awake this late. He was imagining something else—imagining himself that first year with the Symphony, *that* younger mother. And who was to say she was self-contained; why did he picture a navy suit? His recollections of her were dim. She'd been dead 40 years.

And now the brightness, the polished blond wood of the stage and a change in the deep audience murmur—not a cessation, but a pause and a slightly higher pitch. He was used to this. He filed in behind the other bassoonists. They took their seats, settling their seat straps under them, nestling the ends of their horns carefully so as not to bang against the music stands or each other. Cynthia Houseworth was almost four months pregnant, barely showing (not at all under that black dress) and already radiant. She was 35; this was her first child. Provided all went well, she intended (she had told him last month) to take off from late March through the summer. She was a good musician. Certainly it would be strange to take off a few months to do this other thing and come back. Your whole life would be changed. Stephen was always telling him he should consider the lives of women more. "They are fundamentally more complex, Gerald. Consider what it's like to have a child, to grow something in your body and push it out into the world. *That's* power and influence." But Stephen's statements usually smacked of political correctness to Gerald. He watched Cynthia curl her straight blonde hair behind her ear and incline her head toward Leonard, who smiled at her joke. She and Leonard were friendly to Gerald but cautious, deferential. She had never inclined her head toward *him*. Perhaps this was because he had been with the Symphony so long; perhaps it was because of the few times during woodwind sectionals that he'd blown up over something they thought was trivial. Perhaps they wished he was older and would retire. He didn't know. He would have liked Cynthia to incline her head toward him and tell him a joke. Yes, he would have liked that.

Gerald straightened his music. *Scheherazade.* It had been six years since they played it. He would always associate the piece with Roland—an image of Roland asleep on the pull-out couch, the tanned, muscular arm flung over the white pillow....

Now Berkowski, coming across the stage, the familiar lumber and Einsteinian hair (somewhat affected, Gerald thought), the click against the stand, the hush in the audience, a seriousness, and Berkowski looking in the direction of Howard for the tuning *A*, Howard's sour *A*, and the orchestra's slow gathering around that note. A humming *A* and then a disintegration as the musicians tried to get a few riffs in edgewise—scales, trills, passages from the program. Then the *click* again and Gerald forgot his musings and was poised with the instrument, right with the music, where he was most himself.

Everything went as expected. A couple of near misses with the string section, for whatever reason, but not a bad performance. Afterward, Gerald waited twenty minutes for Stephen in the instrument room. He didn't show up. Gerald was not particularly worried; there would probably be a message on his machine at home. Howard Ziesing asked him if he wanted to join some others for a drink, but he declined and took a cab home. The lights were on and everything was as Gerald had left it—why should it be so different after four hours? The answering machine light was blinking—Stephen, saying something had come up and he'd had to pass tonight, and John, who'd forgotten tonight was a concert and he'd be home tomorrow. Everyone had checked in. Gerald watched television without the sound for as long as it took him to drink a glass of scotch, enjoying the quiet, letting it sift around him like a blanket, then turned off the lights one by one and went to bed.

Chapter 4

Herminda saw Mickey come in the kitchen entrance of the cafe just as she was getting off her shift on Saturday. She turned away from the counter abruptly, pretending she hadn't seen him, untying and retying her waitress apron. What was she suddenly so nervous about? she chided herself. They were just going to a movie.

Mickey came around the corner and touched her elbow lightly from behind. "Hi," he said. "You ready?"

He looked different, freshly showered with his hair combed back, wearing a red rugby shirt and jeans that were a little tight. He looked like a college boy, friendly and eager, which made her uncomfortable. She preferred the disheveled, tired Mickey from behind-the-counter.

"Yeah," she said. "I saw you; I'll be out in a minute." Herminda saw his face fall slightly at her impatient tone, but he recovered quickly, smiled, and told her he'd be out back.

In the tiny cafe restroom, Herminda combed her hair back and looked at her face in the mirror. She'd worn a white blouse and jeans with a beaded belt. She put on some eyeliner, and a dab of her sister's perfume behind each ear. Her face was too thin, she thought, unbalanced. Too skinny all around. No breasts. She tried to imagine someone (Mickey) putting his hand on her breast. What a surprise he'd have, she thought. Nothing there, practically. She blew an exasperated puff of air at her reflection. A movie; it was just a movie, she said to herself.

"I thought we'd go to the Fillmore and check out a Clint Eastwood," Mickey said when she got into the red VW Rabbit, which was idling in the alley behind the cafe. "*Unforgiven*. I didn't see it the first time around, did you? Unless you've got something else in mind?"

"No. That's fine," she said, glancing at him and taking in his car. The interior was red, too, and it wasn't new as she had thought when she caught a glimpse of it from the kitchen. There were a couple of matchbox trucks between the seats and a car seat in the back; otherwise, the car was clean. There was a hole where a tape deck would be and plain black mats on the floor— nothing to identify the owner, no medallions or stickers with sayings on them, nothing hanging from the rearview mirror. Herminda didn't have a driver's license and rarely rode in a car. Her mother didn't own one, and although Ricardo had a car, it was always at their cousin's, and it usually wasn't working.

"I don't drive," she said, as if he'd asked her.

"Why not?"

"I don't know. I never learned."

Mickey smiled and tapped her leg lightly. She stiffened. "Well, maybe I can teach you. And sometime," he continued, "I'd like to hear you play."

Herminda pictured herself playing something from *Man of La Mancha* for Mickey, her mouth all distended, her cheeks going in and out.... she definitely did *not* want him to hear her play. What if he were in another room, listening, his ear pressed to a grate like in a confessional? She smirked.

"What's so funny?" Mickey smiled at her.

"Nothing. Nothing."

They drove in silence. Mickey found a parking space and Herminda closed her eyes to avoid seeing the mere inch of space between their car and the one alongside it as Mickey fit the car into a space more suitable for a motorcycle.

"Are you okay?"

"You're a good parker."

He tapped her leg again and smiled.

The previews were already beginning when they went in, and they sat in the first aisle seats they could find. Herminda sat tensely in her seat through the violent opening scene of the movie, where a prostitute in an old-west brothel got knifed by an irate customer. She kept glancing at Mickey from the corner of her eye, but he seemed absorbed in the action, and gradually she was, too. She imagined what it would be like to live with a group of women in a hotel, saving up money to take revenge on the man who cut one of them up. Before, she had only seen Clint as a tough guy in Spanish-version films; it was amusing to see him as a tough guy tamed by a woman whose only part on screen was portrayed by her headstone.

By the end of the movie Herminda felt lost in the action and unsettled when the lights came up and there was Mickey beside her. They watched the credits in silence.

"It's kind of strange," Mickey said when they finally stood up to leave, the last people in the theater. He touched her elbow as if to guide her out to the aisle.

"What's kind of strange?"

"It's strange to go to a movie with someone the first time you go out. I mean, you hardly know them, so you go to a dark room and watch a movie and don't talk. You could drop them off and not know anything more than what you did when you picked them up."

Herminda liked the way he said *the first time you go out.* "I guess that's why people who are married a long time like to go to movies. So they won't *have* to talk," she said. "I don't go to movies much," she added.

"No?"

"No time. No money, usually." Herminda didn't add that when she did go, she went alone and preferred the farthest row at the back of the theater.

Outside, it was dark, and they could see their reflections in the window of a bookstore next to the theater. Mickey seemed very tall, some sort of red-haired gringo basketball giant, and she looked tiny and dark, like an orphan. She stood up straighter and held her head up. Now she looked haughty and defensive, like she was making up for her smallness. There wasn't a way to look right.

Mickey pointed at the window, and for a moment Herminda thought he was noticing their reflection, too. "You want to go in there?" he asked. "They've got desserts at the back, and good coffee."

Herminda hadn't eaten any dinner yet, but she nodded. They meandered to the back of the bookstore and found a small table. Mickey bought them each an espresso and a piece of cheesecake. She liked eating near the books. She'd wished there were music stores that had cafes in them, where you could eat surrounded by musical instruments. But those stores were more utilitarian, more like hardware stores where you went in, purchased the swab or key oil that you needed, and left. The books here were like a cushion, an ambiance, but real—not like the books on the decorative shelves at the cafe, books no one would want to read.

"It's nice here," she said, impulsively.

He smiled. "Why?"

"Why nice?" She was flustered. "Well, it's bright, not like the café. And it's not dark, and smoky, like a bar. I like the books."

"Do you read a lot?"

She shrugged. "No. But I like the books. I mean, think of the hundreds of thousands of conversations in all of them, all around us," she said.

Mickey looked down the fiction aisle and chuckled. "Yeah, with all of them going on it'd sound like a World Series game in here."

"No, I don't mean all of them going at once—just the possibility for all of them, just right there in the book pages, waiting to be read. It makes you think you could have a real conversation yourself, right here."

Mickey's eyes widened and he leaned back, smiling. "Whoa! A real conversation! I don't know if I'm ready for that with you," he said.

Herminda slapped his hand and almost spilled her espresso. "Stop teasing me," she laughed.

"No, really," Mickey said. "I'm good for it, a real conversation—I really am. Are you saying, Dr. Matta, that reality is in books, or that reality is in conversation?"

Herminda rolled her eyes. "Reality is up your...you-know-what...Dr. Kelly," she said impulsively, and blushed.

"Well, yes," Mickey said, with mock consideration, "there is indeed a certain amount of reality right up there. However did you know?" He pretended to look over his shoulder.

Herminda laughed and was grateful for the way Mickey took her embarrassment from her. What would her brother think of him? Ricardo's thin, sulky, handsome frame—always with those

dark plaid, oversize shirts, buttoned to his neck, and big pants—
was like a shadow in her mind. She could never clearly picture
his face. Ricardo would have disdain for Mickey's looks, and for
his self-effacing manner, and would probably be a little jealous
of his managerial status at the café. She looked at Mickey's face,
his thin lips and the spattering of freckles under and over his
nose. He was at least as funny looking as she was. She looked at
the empty espresso cup. She felt as if she'd had a beer.

"I was at the World Series," Mickey was saying, "during the
earthquake—at Candlestick."

"1989."

"'89, yes." Mickey paused, as if wondering where Herminda
might have been then, when she would have been just a baby. "I
was six. I think my parents split up over the fact that my dad
took me and then there was an earthquake."

Mickey had a distant look. Herminda had never been to
Candlestick Park, so she wasn't sure what to imagine. She
pictured a giant, open flying saucer.

"I still do remember it. The game was about to start, and the
whole place was rumbling. It was like the stadium was going to
take off, or something. It was amazing. My dad grabbed me and
picked me up. Later, after they divorced, he told me that he was
thinking as he was holding me there that if he had to go,
everything had been pretty sweet so far. I think about that
sometimes when I take Christopher to a game."

Herminda was impressed that Mickey took his son to games.

"What's your wife like?"

"Christina?"

"Yeah." So his son Christopher was named after his wife.

"She thinks I'm an unambitious, hopeless, tiresome romantic.
In short, she doesn't want to hear about it—*it* being anything

related to me." He shrugged and smiled flatly. "In fact, I was telling her—yeah, probably for the twentieth time—how I loved being in that earthquake with my dad, at the ballgame, and she said she didn't want to be in that life anymore. *That life*, she called it the thing we were supposedly doing together."

Herminda looked at the floor, which needed scrubbing. "What's she doing now?"

He shrugged again. "Honestly, I don't know. She moved up north, to Washington. We don't keep in touch. She gave me full custody of Christopher and a chunk of money, and I took both. So."

Herminda had never known of a father taking a son, and the mother leaving. She was quiet.

"She was a failure of mine, a big failure."

"Why is it your failure? She's the one who left."

Mickey examined the backs of his hands. "Because I was so far from her that I never even knew she was leaving. I was so much in my own world—just me and my baby boy and grad school and one day rolling after the other—that I had no idea where she went, or that she was going at all. I did tell her I was sorry for that. I mean, I'm not taking all the blame. But a good part of it *is* mine. But then you move on. So what about you?"

She wasn't going to let him change the subject. She didn't want to talk about herself; there was nothing, in her opinion, to offer.

"How old was—is—she—Christina?"

"My age, 27. Her birthday's the day after mine."

"Is she pretty?"

Mickey shrugged, and looked away, like he was about to blush. "Pretty enough."

Pretty *enough*, she thought. To fuck and make babies with and lose. Now it was her turn to look away. The two women at the cashier glanced in their direction, and she knew that they wanted to close. "We should get going," she said, and felt his finger lightly tap the back of her hand on the table.

"If you're going to use her prettiness, or whatever you're imagining about her, to keep me away from you....well, I don't know what to say. I guess I wish you wouldn't." She looked at him, surprised. Mickey's face was completely red, as if he were angry. "It's just that...." He noticed the cashiers. The front lights were out. "We *should* get going."

"It's just that what," she continued his sentence when they were on the sidewalk outside the bookstore.

Mickey turned to her. "It's this, Herminda. I've watched you for six months, and I am completely, *completely* attracted to you"—here his voice sped up and his eyes darted toward the curb — "and everything I've seen about you, in you, interests me, and that's why I asked you out, finally." He was looking at her again. "And that's all. So I may as well tell you. I haven't been out with anyone in two years. I'm lousy with women; I say too much. The last one I went out with said I was—how did she put it?— 'a sensitive man with no future'."

He turned away abruptly. Herminda followed his gaze. They were reflected in the bookstore window again, the streetlight behind them. She knew he was seeing their reflection now. This time he didn't look so tall, and she didn't look so much like an orphan. She didn't know what to say to him, or whether he expected her to say anything at all. She didn't feel he was insincere; actually, she wondered whether she had ever heard anyone say anything so sincerely. It was confusing.

"It's confusing," Mickey said, as if following her thought, and laughed. She laughed, too. He put his arm around her shoulder, lightly, and she thought they didn't look so bad together.

They made a date for next Saturday. When he dropped her off he leaned over, stroked her hair with the back of his hand and kissed her, very lightly, on the cheek, and that was it. "Good night," he said.

"Good night." She fumbled with the door handle to get out. Inside, she watched him pull away, the brake lights flashing red as he paused at 23rd Street and turned the corner.

Completely, completely attracted to you, she repeated to herself as she wiped down a table on Monday and filled coffee filters with pre-measured packages of coffee, stacking them for the busy time later in the afternoon. She didn't quite believe what he had said. No one would ever be completely, completely attracted to her, just as she couldn't imagine anyone ever being completely, completely attracted to Mickey. She thought again of how they looked in the bookstore window. She was glad Mickey wasn't working at the same time she was today so she could think about him, in his environment, without him being around. They were oddities; she knew that, and she felt together with him in their oddness.

It was mid-afternoon when the blonde man came in again. Herminda saw him from the window before he came in. He was wearing a red shirt and black jeans and sneakers. She watched as he paused outside and pulled out his wallet, apparently checking to see how much money he had, and then came in. He had the *Chronicle* under his arm. He grinned when he saw her and took a table closer to the kitchen this time. She brought him a menu.

"Hi, again," he said, scooting up to the table.

"How's it going?"

"It's going okay." He patted the newspaper. "Got to find a place to live."

She didn't say anything and started to turn back to her station while he looked at the menu.

"Wait. I know what I want. Turkey—is it fresh turkey breast? not that rolled stuff?—and swiss on pumpernickel. Lettuce and tomatoes, everything. A beer." He squinted over her shoulder at the beer bottle display. Herminda suspected he wore glasses. "No, maybe not. Coffee would be more like it. Yeah, coffee."

"Okay," she said.

But he was quiet during his lunch and didn't try to engage her again. She watched him for a while from behind the counter as he went through the paper with a red pen, circling possibilities, and then two other groups of people came in and distracted her. By the time she had finished bringing the other people their food, the man was ready for his check. He smiled at her as she wrote up the ticket.

"So," she said, "any luck?"

He shrugged. "I've got to find a job, too, if you hear of anything."

"Yeah. Well, you know, you could put up an ad on that bulletin board there," she said, pointing to the wall behind him. "And lots of times there are ads for people looking for roommates."

"I hadn't thought of that. Yeah, I'll definitely do that."

The order-up bell rang.

"How much was my tab?"

"$6.40."

He gave her a ten. "Keep the change."

Herminda was pleased at the tip but felt uneasy taking it. The order bell rang again; Fred was glaring at her from the kitchen.

"I'll be around again soon," the man said. "If you'd keep an eye out for any roommate ads, I'd appreciate it."

Toward the end of her lesson that afternoon, Gerald told her that he wanted her to play with Richard on her own. He had brought up the idea to Richard, who was eager to play with her. (Probably so that he could act like a teacher, she thought. Richard was an ass.) It would be good for her, Gerald said, to work together with someone who wasn't a teacher. Where would they play? she asked. They couldn't play at her house. What would they work on?

"Just go through the duet book," Gerald said. "Piece by piece. Pay attention to him. See what you like and what you don't. In a symphony you don't always *like* everyone you have to perform with. You can get together here sometime, when I'm out."

"I don't know."

"Look, Herminda, you're at least as good as Richard," Gerald said, finally, and that statement made her quiet.

He got up and poured himself a cup of coffee from the thermos on the counter. In seven months he had not given her many compliments. Herminda let this one sink in. After a moment, his back to her, Gerald asked, "So. Did you make it to the concert the other night?"

The inquiry was very casual, but she could tell if she hadn't gone it would've meant something to Gerald—she wasn't sure what—and it made Herminda feel badly that she hadn't brought it up herself, at the beginning of the lesson—to thank him, at least. She nodded vigorously.

"And did you enjoy it?"

"Yes, very good. I mean, very much. Especially *Scheherazade*."

"Yes, that's a favorite. We play it about every six years or so." He turned toward her, sipping his coffee, unreadable.

The seat had been a good one, in the center front, and if she squinted she could see the scuffs on the back of conductor's black shoes. She had watched, absorbed, as the strings filed onstage, and a minute later Gerald and two other bassoonists, and a fat man with his oboe.... At first it had seemed as though everyone was white and middle-aged, but as they warmed up Herminda noticed that one of the flutists and a viola player were black, and the timpani player was young, with a long ponytail, and there were actually several others who appeared to be in their 20's. She tried to picture herself on stage, next to Gerald, but then the conductor came onstage and she directed her attention to him. There was tuning, the wavering into balance, and the first piece was *Scheherazade*. Herminda knew of Rimsky-Korsakov, but she couldn't remember if she'd ever heard *Scheherazade*. There was a microphone stand next to the podium with a very thin boom to over the bassoons, and she understood why when Gerald opened the second movement with a beautiful solo which might have gotten lost if there weren't a mic. Her vision of Gerald was almost as if she were seeing through a zoom lens, his face strained and contorted but somehow natural, and the solo went through her, playful and clear, and the skin on her arms prickled. Then the oboes joined in, and then the strings.

"That solo was beautiful," she said.

Gerald smiled, slowly. There was a loud knock at the front door then, and he excused himself to answer it.

After the concert, Herminda had gone backstage. A burly man at the stage entrance looked her over and let her through when she said she was a student of one of the orchestra members and gave Gerald's name. Musicians were leaving in small groups from an open door down the hall, talking and laughing. Herminda saw the two bassoonists, recognizable by their long cases, and she wondered how old the woman bassoonist was. How long had she been playing? She watched for Gerald but didn't see him. Finally, she came further down the hall and looked into the instrument room. There were only a few musicians left. She saw Gerald's open bassoon case with the pristine blue velvet interior first, and then she saw him. He was sitting on a bench by himself, hunched over with his back to her, the neck of his white shirt wet with perspiration. He seemed very tired. She almost called his name, but Gerald stood up suddenly and began putting on his jacket, and Herminda backed out of the doorway and retreated down the hall. A couple of minutes later she saw him come out, his black coat buttoned. He checked his watch and peered down the dark hallway, but did not see her, then pushed the bar on the Exit door, which closed behind him with a hydraulic hush.

She wouldn't know what to say to him, she'd thought, and he was on his way somewhere.

Herminda heard talking at the front door, and someone came in. Then Gerald appeared at the kitchen door and said, "I think that's okay for today, Herminda," in an apologetic voice.

"Yeah, sure. We were pretty much done."

While she was packing up her bassoon, Herminda heard more talking. She'd meant to ask Gerald after the lesson where he got his reed-making materials, and whether he would help her learn to make her own reeds. (She did not really see how she could ever sculpt a piece of cane down to an object that felt so familiar in her mouth. It had to be just right. She would never be able to get it just right.) But she wasn't going to ask anything with someone else here. She put the envelope with Gerald's lesson money on the table, wondering whether he would deduct the fifteen minutes they didn't do, and went out the swinging kitchen door with her case, practically bumping into the blonde man she had served two hours before at the Café Del Sol.

"Oh!" he said, "it's you."

"Yeah," she said, startled, "it's me."

"You know each other?" Gerald asked. He stood by the sliding glass window, smoking. He seemed nervous.

"Well, no. She made me a cappuccino—a couple of cappuccinos."

"He was at the café where I work," Herminda explained stiffly.

"Well, Roland, this is Herminda Matta, a student of mine; and Herminda, this is Roland Staple, a friend of mine."

Roland grinned at her and put out his hand. "Actually, I'm his second cousin."

"My second cousin," Gerald repeated.

"But perhaps I'd rather be a friend."

Herminda shook Roland's hand, which was rough and dry.

"Herminda. What does that mean?" Roland asked.

She shrugged. "It doesn't mean anything in English. Some people think it's like 'Mindy' in English."

"Oh." Roland was looking curiously at her. "Nice to meet you officially, Herminda," Roland said. His accent was very good. She wondered if he spoke Spanish. "Geez, how do you lug a bassoon around?"

"She is ingenious," Gerald commented.

Herminda didn't like the way Gerald said she was ingenious.

"I'll be going," she said, awkwardly, retrieving her luggage tote from under the coat stand where she usually left it. Herminda felt the two men watching her as she strapped on her bassoon case, waiting tensely for her to go. What was between them? She imagined there was a long answer for that, and she wasn't sure she wanted to know.

Chapter 5

Gerald first met Roland six years ago, when Roland had hitchhiked to the city from Southern California. It was late summer, no fog. On Gerald's doorstep the late afternoon sun came in at an angle across the top of Roland's head, his longish hair so blond that Gerald had to squint to make out his face. Roland carried a duffel bag in one hand, and a shopping bag in the other.

"Gerald Poulin? I'm Roland Staple." He dropped the duffel bag and put out his hand. "Your cousin."

Gerald had known who Roland was before he said it—he looked like old photos of Aunt Jeanette. Through the years Gerald had received letters and occasional calls from Jeanette; she had managed to keep track of her grandson through the foster homes. Reaching her daughter had been harder, and the last he'd heard Jeanette didn't know where her daughter was.

He invited him in, and Roland set his things down by the door. "I was in town," he said casually, tossing his head slightly to get his hair off his forehead, "and I thought I'd stop by to meet you. Finally."

Was there the slightest tinge of incrimination in Roland's voice, Gerald wondered, that he hadn't ever gone to San Diego to see his only cousin or Roland, her son?

"Well," Gerald had said, moving toward the living room, "this is very interesting."

Roland eyed the living room, taking in the furniture, the tape equipment, the music stand. "I hope it's not a bad time."

"No—not bad. I'm just—uh, fixing some dinner—I eat early—maybe you want to join me. It's light—I'm trying to lose weight." Gerald tapped his stomach self-consciously.

"Oh, anything'd be great," Roland said, looking relieved. "I haven't eaten all day." He smiled and shrugged at this admission. Gerald tried to keep from staring—Roland looked so much like Jeanette must have looked when she was his age. The same blue-gray eyes and the mouth with the upward tilt, very falsely giving the impression that she was always cheerful, determined. Gerald knew, suddenly, that Roland was here with no particular aim in mind, and his guardian, if there was one, probably didn't know where he was.

Gerald was having a salad, but he pulled out some deli roast beef and made Roland a large sandwich, and a second one after that, which Roland ate hungrily. Roland watched as Gerald poured a scotch; he almost offered Roland one, but remembered that there was juice and soda in the refrigerator. He was glad he had gone shopping. He hadn't eaten at home with anyone in a long time. It was odd that he felt comfortable with Roland.

"Do you ever see your mother? Veronica?" The name was strange on his tongue. Veronica had run away when she was a teenager and ended up in San Diego shortly after Gerald moved to California. He hadn't seen his cousin in almost 20 years.

Roland shrugged and said he hadn't lived with Veronica (he called his mother by her first name) for a couple of years now, and that it seemed to work out better for both of them that way. "I was in foster homes. You probably knew that." He paused and gave Gerald a surveying look. "I didn't even really know about her until I was five. And when I moved back in with her, neither of us knew what to do." Roland shrugged again, finishing his sandwich. "Veronica's very schitzy," he said. "You don't know what she'll do next."

Gerald nodded. That was an accurate assessment, he thought.

Talking with Roland was easy. His voice was quiet and friendly, and his smile was quick. Although Gerald had correctly calculated his age, he seemed much older than 16. He seemed like an adult, at least 20 or 21. When he left Veronica's house, he said, he'd lived with "friends." He'd even spent a few months with the man who claimed to be his father, but that ended when the man started bringing different women home, and now Roland doubted whether the man was really his father after all.

He stood up, cleared off the plates, and took them to the sink. Gerald moved to get up. "Please," Roland said. "It was a great meal, let me at least take care of the dishes." Someone had trained him, Gerald thought. While he cleaned the kitchen he asked Gerald questions about himself—what he did, how long he'd lived here, and so forth. Roland listened quietly as he dried the dishes and put them away. As he talked, Gerald watched Roland. His red tee-shirt had a diagonal streak of dirt across it. His legs were long and thin in tight, worn jeans.

Roland finished, and dried his hands. "Do you mind if I smoke?" he asked, noting the blue ceramic bowl where Gerald laid out his day's allotment of cigarettes. Gerald shook his head. "Merits," Roland said, looking at the cigarette as though the brand would tell him something important about Gerald, squinting slightly as he took his first draw. He obviously smoked regularly. His arms were slender and tanned, but muscular, and his hands were wide, with round, bitten fingernails.

"What are you going to do in San Francisco?" Gerald asked.

Roland looked at him and sighed. "I suppose by now you've guessed," he said, "that I have no idea what I'm doing here, and that no one knows I'm here. Things weren't so great where I was staying, and I couldn't get a decent job. I'm too young." He shrugged and snuffed out his cigarette. "I hitchhiked up here."

Gerald was puzzled and pleased by this straightforwardness.

"Don't you think you should let someone know?"

Roland crossed his arms and stared at the table, almost pouting. It was the first time since he'd arrived that he looked his age. Then he uncrossed his arms. "Yes," he said. "I should let them know—the people I was staying with."

"What about school?"

Roland smiled, self-satisfied. "I passed my GED in January. I hated school. Most parts of it, anyway. I didn't fit in." He glanced up to see how Gerald was taking all this. "And in So- Cal everything's so ridiculous. It's Beach Boy-a-Rama, if you know what I mean."

Gerald didn't know what he meant. He had a mental picture of blond boys—not unlike Roland, actually—wearing fluorescent colored suits and riding the waves on surfboards. On the beach, of course, girls waited and watched in bikinis. His image was heterosexual. Of course, he had only been down to LA twice.

Gerald had put coffee on and when it was ready they moved into the living room. It got dark as they sat in chairs which they turned toward the window. Gerald had liked being there with Roland then. They both smoked, and neither of them moved to turn on the light.

Gerald knew Veronica had had a baby because she'd called him, collect, from the hospital in San Diego. It was twilight when she called, sixteen years ago. He had just gotten the job with the Symphony and rented the flat, a couple of old stuffed chairs on the hardwood floor, a bed, a desk made of a board over two filing cabinets. His stereo was on the floor, his albums in crates all along the east wall of the living room. The look of the place was as clear as if he'd moved in yesterday. Why was his mind so sharpened for certain moments? He had been sitting on his practice chair, looking out the window over the dilapidated deck toward downtown. He remembered twisting the phone cord around his wrist and letting it go as Veronica talked.

Veronica was hysterical, claiming her boyfriend had made her shoot up and Gerald was the only one who could get her baby back. *I hardly know her*, he had thought. The few times he had seen his cousin, she was like her mother, stubborn and blond and attractive, but Veronica was ten years younger than him, and Gerald had little in common with her. It took fifteen minutes on the phone to decipher that she had been using heroin when she was pregnant, and the boy was born addicted. The hospital had put the infant on methadone, unsure of brain damage, and a foster family had been notified for when the baby was discharged. Gerald talked to Veronica for a while, and eventually she calmed down enough to give him the number of the hospital, and to tell him that the baby was beautiful; his name was Roland.

As soon as he got off the phone, he called his aunt to tell her.

"She's like...someone I've never known," Jeanette said, finally. "Like someone I've never known, and never will." Her voice sounded older than he'd ever heard it, worn out.

"I could go down there, to San Diego," he said, reluctantly, but Jeanette told him not to.

"I'll deal with it," she said.

"Let me know if there's anything...I can do."

Gerald untwisted the phone cord from his arm, which he'd wound all the way up to his elbow. His arm was red—he had unknowingly wound the cord so tight—and he watched the skin slowly lighten and become pale again. It had grown dark outside, and it was beginning to rain. He turned on the lamp and looked around his living room with relief. He wouldn't have to go to San Diego. He wouldn't have to deal with what he didn't want to understand—these people, his distant family. He wouldn't have to look into Veronica's haggard face, or see her baby, Roland, as he imagined him, screaming, all tangled up in tubes.

He looked over at Roland on the couch. Over the years he had wondered about him. Jeanette had given various reports on his whereabouts, and now here he was, a young man.

"Your grandmother helped me out when I was at the conservatory in Boston. She used to come to all my concerts."

"Yeah. Jeanette. She sends me checks. They always catch up with me, and they always come in handy." Roland chuckled and then stopped, as though he thought he might be offensive.

"She died last year."

"Oh," Roland said. "I never met her."

"I think she saw you once, when you were an infant."

"That doesn't count."

"No, you're right. That doesn't count." Jeanette should never have had a baby, and her daughter should never have had a baby. "She left me a lot of her things, though. The piano. That antique table...." Gerald pointed across the dark room.

"Well. That was nice of her," Roland said simply.

They looked northeast out the sliding glass doors onto the city. The sky was deep dark blue, like it was when the wind had blown the rim of pollution away and the Sacramento Valley was cool enough that fog didn't form.

"You have a beautiful place," Roland said, breaking the quiet, at the same time that Gerald said, "Do you need a place to stay?"

They answered each other at the same time, too. "Thank you," Gerald said, and Roland said, "Yes."

They both smiled. "Could I stay here a few days?"

"Sure," Gerald said. "But call those people you were staying with and let them know where you are."

"I will."

Roland stayed with Gerald for six weeks. It worked out fairly well at first. Roland was skilled at adapting to other people's routines and making himself fit in. When Gerald was out at morning rehearsals, he'd leave some cash and Roland would buy groceries, the items and brands Gerald liked. (He'd looked through all the cupboards.) He cleaned the place. When Gerald gave lessons, he made himself scarce. He made dinner. After dinner they would sit in the dark and talk, and Gerald found himself telling him about music, performing, about meeting his grandmother Jeanette and her latest boyfriend after concerts.

Roland seemed to enjoy the stories. He was more reluctant to talk about his own life, and there were certain gaps he didn't fill in. Gerald especially wondered about the people Roland had been staying with the past couple years, but he didn't press him. He enjoyed his company; he enjoyed having someone around. He had been alone a long time.

"You'd better watch yourself," Stephen had said to Gerald after dinner one evening when Roland was in the other room. Stephen's tone was only half-kidding.

"Okay, okay! You'd better watch *me*, then," Stephen had responded to Gerald's incredulous look.

Then one night, just after two weeks, Gerald was on the edge of sleep, and he felt Roland sit down at the end of the bed. He heard him breathing.

"Gerald?" Roland said.

He rolled over slowly.

"Can I sleep with you?" he asked. Gerald didn't have his contact lenses in and he couldn't see clearly. Roland's voice was sad and strange. Gerald didn't think. He just moved over on the bed, and Roland crawled in. They both lay in the bed for several minutes, quiet and tense, waiting. And then finally, from sheer tension, Gerald leaned over him, and put his hand on Roland's chest, just lightly, and they moved toward each other. Roland's hand was on his cock, and the next few minutes were a flurry of hunger and nerves. Afterward they lay close together, saying nothing, the sheets tangled at the foot of the bed. Gerald thought of the few times he'd had sex before—the cellist when he'd been at the conservatory. (They'd spent a few awkward afternoons together in that basement apartment in Cambridge, both of them inexperienced.) And then Gerald had gotten the job in San Francisco and moved. Since living here, he'd had two boyfriends, both older men with whom he felt safe. He was the one who broke it off both times, and now *he* was the older man.

Where could this lead? As he stroked Roland's hair in the dim room, he realized that this was the first time Roland had seen him without his toupee.

The next night Roland came to his room again. This time Roland rolled onto his stomach. Gerald was afraid to have sex this way; it felt too violent. He ran his hand down Roland's smooth back. "I don't know," he whispered.

"Please," Roland said.

Afterward they were quiet, lying curled together like spoons, Roland's arms around him from behind. Gerald could not remember feeling this way before. He felt soft, as though he might cry, but also energized. They lay together a while longer, and then Roland went back to the living room.

After that, Gerald went to Roland, and over the next few weeks they made a strange ritual. They each said goodnight and Gerald went to his room, leaving the door open. He would wait until he heard Roland pull out the sofa bed, and heard him climb in. Then he would take off his clothes and stand in the doorway until Roland lifted the covers and patted the sheet gently. There was a comfort with Roland that surprised him. It was a physical comfort, though, and a distinct feeling that any talk would shatter the ease. When Gerald tried to speak, Roland would put a finger on his lips, as though talk and sex had nothing to do with each other, and he wouldn't let one invade the other. Roland was distant, but seemed to enjoy it—even, to require it. His body, so young and so lean, was exquisite to Gerald, and when he was lying with him he thought of nothing but Roland's body and his own desire. It was brand new to him. It was as though they reversed roles, and Roland was the older of them. Certainly, Roland was in control. Afterward, lying in the dark, or with a candle burning, they would lie quietly until Roland said, "I need to sleep." He couldn't sleep with him (Gerald later wondered if he could sleep with anyone), and Gerald would go back to his own bed. During the day, Roland was gone more often. Gerald left him extra money—for clothes, for a haircut. He thought about Roland while he practiced, and at rehearsals.

And then Roland was seeing someone else, or maybe many others. He looked pretty good, using makeup to cover his acne.

His blond hair was cut trim, and he'd bought nice clothes. He had good taste and spent Gerald's money well: tight jeans, white shirts, a pair of beautiful black wool slacks. He went out at night. Wide awake, his door open all the time now, Gerald would hear him come in. He would hear the bed open out, a sigh, his pants dropping to the floor. And then he would get up out of bed, humiliated even as he was also driven, and stand in the doorway. The living room was still. Then Roland, naked, would roll over. "Gerald," he said, "I'm tired."

Gerald cleared his throat. "Sure," he said. "Sure." And he lay in bed all night, awake, and he knew he was hooked.

He still worked; he still practiced his bassoon, and he knew then that if he played while he felt this way, he would play no matter what happened to him. Practicing was something, anyway, something physical besides the way he went through the living room after Roland left each day, looking through his clothes stacked neatly in the duffel bag, smelling them, looking for evidence of other men. Whatever Roland was doing, he was careful and pristine about it.

Then, suddenly, as if he knew Gerald was looking for it, Roland wasn't careful. He left a vial of cocaine and a bottle of amylnitrate on the end table, along with some hundred-dollar bills and a number scribbled on the back of a receipt. It was almost as though he set it up to force Gerald to confront him.

And what would he confront him about? Roland was almost 17; Gerald was 46. Roland had seen, had been with every part of his body. Gerald was a fool. He was humiliated as he asked him, but he forced himself to. He asked Roland if they were lovers.

Roland had leaned back on the sofa and smiled open-mouthed, as if ready to laugh, but he saw Gerald's face and stopped. Perhaps he was thinking of the flat, of continuing to stay there, and the money—although by now he probably had money from other men. "Lovers," he said. "Do you mean, like, are we in love with each other? Is that what you mean?"

"I'd like to know how you take the word," Gerald said, beginning to perspire.

"I've enjoyed having sex with you," he said, and shrugged. "I guess that's lovers."

"That's past-tense," Gerald said.

"What?"

"You said you 'have enjoyed.'" Roland looked confused. "I guess you've enjoyed sex a lot these past few weeks," Gerald said. "I guess you've enjoyed the money, too. I see you're earning a bit on your own." These last words came out in a flurry.

Roland flushed. He looked more like a boy than Gerald had ever seen him and turned his head away angrily. "Well, *fuck* you, Gerald! *Fuck* you! You invite me to stay—who knows what was in your brain—and you fuck me every night—a fucking *old man*, that's what you are. Your whole life's in your head, or written out in...*notes*." He turned to Gerald, furious. "And now— and now you think you're taking care of the poor *boy*. Well, *fuck* you!" He stood up. His face paled back to normal and his voice lowered, "Who's taking care of who, Gerald? That's what I'd like to know. You aren't any different than anyone, Gerald. C'mon, fuck me. You'd like to right now, wouldn't you." He moved toward Gerald as if he had a weapon.

And he was right. Gerald would've liked to have fucked him right then, grabbed him.... "Leave, Roland," he said. "Leave now."

"No problem," Roland said, turning away abruptly. "No problem," he repeated. "I'm used to leaving."

Gerald had stayed in the next few days, practicing several hours at a time, leaving Roland's things where they were in the bathroom and living room. That was the spring the symphony was playing *Scheherazade*, and Gerald played as if he were making up stories to prolong his life. Roland was in his mind, but he did not think about him; he thought of the music; he worked on the solos, on coming in exactly right, on the vibrato in the section where he played absolutely alone. He practiced, but there was no pleasure in it.

After Roland left, Gerald found himself thinking of the first times they'd had sex. Did it seem like Roland knew what he was doing after that first night? Had he been a prostitute in San Diego? It wasn't as if Roland wasn't experienced, Gerald told himself, angrily. As if he had hurt him, when actually it was more likely the opposite. "More likely"? he asked himself. Christ, didn't he even know whether he was hurt or not, jealous or not? He was so much older than Roland, and he knew nothing.

Gerald thought of his hand, that had first pressed against Roland's chest, as though it had its own life separate from himself. He found himself looking at it in odd places—during a lesson, reading a book. He thought of how one gesture could change his life so, could make him want a lover so badly. He wanted to tell Roland this before he left, but he couldn't. Roland was packing to leave. Gerald stood in the doorway and watched him stuff his things into the duffel bag. Roland looked tired.

"I'm sorry that things turned out...like this," Gerald said. "I feel— if there's anything you need, Roland..."

He looked at Gerald with that new ironic look, or was it new? Had he had that expression when he came and Gerald didn't see it? "Don't worry, Gerald. It's just *fucking*. If it hadn't been you, it would've been someone else. You've been very...generous with me," he said, with an odd smile, throwing the last of his clothes into the bag. He was going to stay with the other man for "a while," he said. Gerald wondered if the other man did cocaine, or supplied it, or any other drugs Roland was interested in.

Yes, Gerald finally decided, it was obvious he was both hurt and jealous, and completely in lust with his cousin. Even then, those things seemed forgivable, so incredibly small in the world. Gerald was sure that Roland didn't think about those nights with him. When he offered the only thing he probably knew to offer, Gerald took it. *Was* it an offering? No, it was payment, and the fact that he didn't recognize the payment as payment, and kept coming back for more when Roland thought the debt he owed was paid was the most humiliating realization Gerald had ever had.

It wasn't lost on him how things come around, a sort of living circle of sharps and flats. One thing he'd begun to understand was that telling the story, giving your confession, wasn't absolution. There wasn't absolution. You could tell the story over and over and change nothing. There were so many layers to honesty, and when you thought you'd found some sort of relief, some face of your own you could accept, you found another level where you'd tricked yourself. There were things in your life that were just done. You could put them away; you could attempt to tell them away, but they didn't go away; they were a sort of chemical waste with an undetermined half-life, and everything— the way you worked and loved—depended on how you dealt with what you had to discard.

And now, past it, Gerald was still in it, and when he thought about Roland he realized the worst thing, that which Roland still held him in greatest contempt for, is the way Gerald didn't, or couldn't, or wouldn't accept himself as ordinary.

Shortly after Roland left, Gerald had met John in the produce market he went to regularly, down on Mission Street. He'd seen John there a few times before, looking uncomfortable in his suit in the midst of the Latin mothers and their trails of children, and the organic punk kids with their chain-adorned canvas sneakers and hair dyed as if to imitate the fruit. "I'm trying to diet—to eat better," John said sheepishly the second time Gerald saw him and he realized Gerald was watching him pick through the apricots. Gerald was embarrassed to be caught watching him, so he just smiled and moved away.

Gerald thought it was the fourth time he saw him—this time in the neighborhood, at Bell Market—that he asked John out. Again, it was in the produce section (now they joked with each other, Oh darling, there among the peaches and apricots, there among the *fruit...*) and he watched John before he finally spoke. John was a burly man, over six feet tall. His hair was thick and black, although now that he'd stopped dying it, it was coming in gray. He was most comfortable in a suit (even in public school his mother made him wear little bow ties each day to school), usually black or dark blue, and thick, expensive wingtip shoes. He had about a hundred ties.

"Hello," Gerald said. His palms began to sweat.

"Hello?" John said, puzzled, and for a moment Gerald thought maybe he had made a big mistake, and the man was straight. Then his face relaxed and he recognized Gerald. "Oh, hello! We must stop meeting like this."

John chuckled, his face flushed, and put his hand out, and Gerald felt so grateful that he forgot to wipe the perspiration off his hand. John glanced briefly at Gerald's hand as he shook it, and Gerald apologized; then John laughed and then they were both laughing. "I've been meaning to ask you if you'd like to go out for coffee," Gerald said, finally.

"Now?" John asked and looked at his watch.

"Oh, well, it doesn't have..."

"Sure, why not? I don't have to be back at the office until 1:30 anyway."

At 1:30 John called the real estate office to say he wouldn't be back that afternoon. He told Gerald he had some time coming. They sat and talked all afternoon and walked into the Mission District and had an early dinner in a Thai restaurant at the end of 24th Street. Gerald hadn't ever met anyone he felt so easy with. They sat at a small table by the window. The light shifted on the pink tablecloth and suddenly it was dark outside and he was telling John about Roland.

John stubbed out his cigarette. "And so now you feel like you owe him something."

"Well, yes, I guess."

"Like what? Money?"

"I had thought of that."

"So you're going to give him money because you think you are responsible for his 'loss of innocence,' as you've called it."

Gerald didn't say anything.

"Gerald, it sounds to me as though he set you up. I mean, perhaps he didn't have full intentions when he arrived, but he saw who you are and how you are, and it probably seemed like a good situation. And the best thing is he didn't even have to ask."

Gerald sighed, and looked out the window.

"He's my cousin, my second cousin."

"Well, Jesus, it's not like he's your brother, or your son. Point of fact: who came into whose room?" John often sounded like a lawyer. Actually, he had his law degree. He said you never knew when it would come in handy.

He made Gerald smile.

"I should have turned on a light, gotten up out of bed to talk to him...."

"C'*mon*, Gerald," John said. For a moment they looked at each like two people who knew what scarcity was, and then they looked away. Gerald didn't see him again for a week and called him at the office. They went out again, several times, although they met and left each other publicly. Finally, after the first performance that spring, Gerald invited him over and he stayed the night. John told him he'd had the test—negative. Up close, he was nervous and blundering and apologetic, and Gerald saw that, like himself, John had not had many lovers. Where Gerald was uncomfortable in public, John was uncomfortable in private. Gerald told him he had never been tested, and that if he wanted he would get the test, and they would not make love tonight. But John had condoms, which he took shyly from his briefcase. Gerald laughed. Afterward, both of them lay awake in the dark. John pressed the tiny light of his watch every half hour or so, checking the time. Gerald was moved by his nervousness; he thought of Roland, of the pleasure of skin finally as tangible to him as music. However ugly it had become there was a way in which Roland had led him to John, and he felt grateful.

When Roland showed up at his doorstep during Herminda's lesson, Gerald wasn't surprised. He looked good, his hair cut short, a dark tan obscuring his acne scars. His clothes were new—a white cotton shirt half open, and khaki slacks. Like the first time he'd arrived, he had a duffel bag over his shoulder. "Hello, Gerald." Roland stood on the step.

"Come in," Gerald said simply.

Roland left his bag by the door, as if to show he had another place to stay.

Gerald went into the kitchen to tell Herminda he thought the lesson was over and found himself lighting a cigarette. When she came out of the kitchen with her horn, Gerald was surprised to see she and Roland had met. Obviously, he hadn't been Roland's first stop in the city. Roland cheerfully directed the conversation toward her. This irritated Gerald; he didn't know why. *Waifs*, he found himself thinking, looking at the two of them. As if she heard his thought, Herminda gave Gerald a scrutinizing glance, but otherwise remained her unreadable self as she strapped up her bassoon and said her goodbyes.

He and Roland weren't alone for more than fifteen minutes before John came by as he usually did for a drink after work. He was still wearing his suit and looked with interest at the young blonde man on the couch. "I've got company," Gerald said. "John, Roland. Roland, John. We're just having a drink, and I bet you'd like one, too," Gerald said.

"Yes, I would." He pecked Gerald on his forehead.

John sat down across from Roland; Gerald poured another scotch. He was beginning to perspire, and his scalp felt itchy under the toupee. John knew about Roland, but that didn't matter; he still felt nervous.

Conversation flowed easily. John talked to Roland about property values in the city. "Wow, I can't believe things are that expensive," Roland said. "I've been hanging out in Santa Monica the past few months, and everything's outrageous there, too." He was drinking scotch.

Gerald sat down on the couch with John and said nothing. "Santa Monica?" John asked.

Roland glanced at Gerald, then back at John. "Yeah." He gave a quick sigh. "It's really beautiful there. I met someone in San Diego who had a really beautiful place, and I couldn't pass up the offer to stay there a few months. The beaches are incredible."

John looked at Gerald.

"Well, okay." Roland saw the look and sighed again, this time annoyed.

"*Okay*, Gerald." His voice took on a mustered firmness, and he faced Gerald, clenching his glass. He took a small sip of the scotch. "I quit school. I couldn't stand it. It had nothing to do with my life. I had to quit, Gerald. I *will* pay you back your money."

After Roland left his place, six years ago, they hadn't spoken for almost a year when Roland called him. They arranged to have lunch, and the meeting was oddly pleasant, like the first dinner they'd had when Roland had shown up at his doorstep. They talked of Roland's job in an office in the Federal Building; he was living with roommates in the Haight. Gerald told him about John, and Roland seemed happy for him. It was as though they'd forgiven each other.

They met again a couple of weeks later, and then Roland told him that he was quitting his job and moving to Santa Barbara, maybe going to school. He was almost 18; he had his GED, after all, and he didn't want to keep being a mailroom clerk all his life. He wanted to know if Gerald would loan him some money for tuition if he was accepted at the University of California. Gerald figured Roland had known he was quitting his job when they'd had lunch, but didn't want to appear to be asking for help before they had reconciled. Oddly enough, Gerald didn't feel angry about it.

"I'd be working, too—part-time at least—and maybe I can get financial aid," Roland said. He was earnest in his request. Maybe school would give him the chance he needed.

"You get enrolled, and show me your schedule, and I'll help you."

"I'm resolved to help him," Gerald said to John over dinner that night. Roland was leaving town in two weeks, with the plan of working through the summer and getting himself acquainted with Santa Barbara and starting school in the fall. *If* he was accepted.

"I'd say more like *absolved* to help him," John commented. "How do you know he'll pay you back? Are you writing out a note?"

"I'm not loaning him the money. I'm going to give it to him."

"I see."

"It's not enough for full tuition."

"That's almost worse. It's an excuse for him to not make it. 'I couldn't get all the money for tuition,' he could say. At any time."

"You are incredibly cynical."

"Yes, I am," John said, cutting his steak. John was an excellent cook, with midwestern tastes.

"Worse than me."

"Yes." He smiled shyly at Gerald.

"I don't know whether to like it or not."

"You don't have to like it or not like it." They were getting to know each other more all the time.

"Look. You're an adult, Roland," Gerald said quietly now. "You don't have to justify anything to me. It was a gift, not a loan."

Roland grunted.

"Well," John said, putting his hands on his thighs. "You guys obviously have a few things to talk about, and I have a house to show in an hour. So, I think I'll be going." He stood up, leaned over and shook Roland's hand. Then he put his hand on Gerald's shoulder. "Call me later."

Gerald smiled at his back as he left.

Roland and Gerald sat in the living room for a few moments, the afternoon light dimming. "So. What does *he* know?" Roland asked.

"About you?"

"Yeah."

"He knows about that time."

Roland leaned back noisily on the couch. "You're lucky, Gerald, you know. All this..." he nodded toward the room, "and someone who loves you like that."

"I am extraordinarily lucky."

"Don't talk British to me," Roland snapped, sitting up abruptly, and then his face softened, almost sad. "You know what I'm going to ask. Can I stay a while?" he asked.

Gerald's body tightened. Of course he'd known Roland was going to ask, from the moment he saw him on the doorstep an hour ago, but he hadn't let himself think forward. A younger Roland would have tried to make him comfortable with the request, by saying, perhaps, "Don't worry; I won't try to seduce you." Gerald was glad Roland just let the question hang in the silence for a moment. Where else could he stay for a couple of weeks? Stephen's? Gerald thought of Stephen's narrow, dark apartment, and the trays of medication on the kitchen counter. No, he could stay here. For a limited time.

"Okay."

"Just until I get a job."

"Sure."

"You're probably wondering what happened."

"Yes."

"I've been wandering around a bit since I quit school. Even made it to New York."

Gerald didn't answer.

"I lived with this guy Craig in Santa Barbara. He was beautiful," Roland said, a bit chastened by Gerald's silence. "Head of his own advertising firm. I loved his place." Roland had finished his drink and looked out the window. He lifted his glass. "Mind if I have another?"

Gerald shook his head. Roland walked over to the counter and poured some more scotch into his glass. "I like it straight," he said, when he saw Gerald watching.

"You like beauty and success."

"Oh, Christ, get off it, Gerald. You like it well enough, as I recall."

"Say whatever you want, Roland. Say it all."

"There's nothing to say."

They were quiet again. Gerald wondered what Roland would do in the city this time.

"He kicked me out—Craig. He accumulates boys, apparently, and I was getting too old."

"Are you...doing anything?"

Roland eyed him, tossing his head as if to get his hair off his face. "I'm clean. I'm clean, just a joint now and then. And this." He lifted his glass of scotch.

"How's your mother?"

"I haven't heard from her. I don't know where she is. I don't care."

Gerald wiped the sweat from his palm onto his thigh.

"Look, Gerald. It's not important. She was an addicted slut, and she's been out of my life for almost longer than I can remember. I'm 22 now."

Gerald looked out the window, then back at him. The light over the stove shone through Roland's white shirt, silhouetting his muscular body underneath it. He was an adult. "Yes. I know."

"What I need," Roland said, sounding suddenly cheerful, "is a job, some money, and some Chinese take-out." He came into the living room with his drink and grinned at Gerald and put a hand briefly on his shoulder like John had done earlier. Out of the corner of his eye Gerald could see Roland's familiar fingers, long and sturdy, still like a teenager's, with bitten nails.

They sat together in the living room. The early winter fog was sifting through the downtown buildings. Gerald felt softened by the scotch. Perhaps John could help get Roland a job or would know of something. "Do you type? I can't remember."

"Of course I type. Isn't that what all of us faggots do? Play bassoon and type?" Roland laughed.

Gerald smiled at him and pointed to his jacket. "There's forty dollars in it. And the keys to the Honda. Don't wreck it. Call the Hong Kong for take-out. The number's by the phone. I'm going to practice. Don't bother me for a couple hours."

"Don't worry, Gerald. I know you need your practice." He winked at him.

Gerald went into the dark bedroom. It was chilly. He turned the knob on the old steam radiator and in a moment it began to clank and hiss. It was the lull between concerts and he didn't need to practice as much as usual, but he wanted to. Just some scales, some basics. The bassoon case was on the bed, and even though he usually practiced in the front room he took off his toupee and put the horn together in the dark. He liked the dark, mostly, and when he was working on a difficult passage he often memorized it and played it in the dark. It was as though the notes were clearer then.

Chapter 6

Herminda only saw Mickey once in the three days before Thanksgiving—long enough for him to say, "We still on for Saturday?" and she said yes, and he smiled and waved at her and headed out the back door of the cafe to his car. She was aware of counting the days. Three days until Thanksgiving, then Friday, and all day Saturday to get through. She couldn't think specifically of what their next date would be like; she focused on how much time there was before it.

She would have liked to practice, but she was at her uncle's shop until late on Wednesday, and today everyone would be hanging around for the holiday. "Everyone" meant her sisters, Elena and Silvia, and her mother. Her uncle José usually went to his in-laws' in San Jose for dinner, and although the five of them would not have increased the dinner by much, Lorena Matta and her children had never been to dinner there and she refused to ask for an invitation. "It's better this way—not so crowded...so crazy," she'd say. "And José —I see him every day." But she was obviously stung that they didn't invite her family. José would stop by to see her later in the evening. And Ricardo—who knew whether he'd show up or not.

"Ricardo came by the shop yesterday," her mother said early on Thursday morning. She and Herminda had both gotten up early to put the turkey in. Elena was at her fiancé's, and Silvia had been out late the night before and was sleeping in. "He said he'd come for dinner."

Herminda knew what that meant. At about one in the afternoon she'd have to walk over to her cousin's on Alabama Street and get Ricardo, and she hated doing that.

She drank her coffee and watched her mother stuff the turkey that her sisters demanded every Thanksgiving. "American babies," she said every year. "Got to have their turkey." At 40, Lorena Matta had shrunk and settled into herself, stocky and dark, appearing much older than she was. This morning she wore an old blue dress with a apron tied around it. She had rinsed her hair with an auburn color that didn't look right with her skin, but Herminda resolved not to say anything. Her movements were quick and efficient, just like at the produce shop where she could separate the bruised from the good in a bin of fruit faster than anyone, even José. And Lorena Matta was enterprising; she knew just when to bag the overripe produce and sell it cheap to the older women who came by every morning.

José worked his sister too hard and did not appreciate her, but Herminda had never heard her say anything against him. Certainly the fact that he owned the building and had let them live practically free since she arrived from New York with four small children under the age of 6 had something to do with that. José also paid his sister a small allowance from the produce shop (he paid Herminda minimum wage by the hour, deducting a small amount each check for the loan on the bassoon) and all the produce she wanted. Lorena Matta's life was simple: she had work, and church (Mass at least twice a week, and socializing with other women from the church), and her Spanish-language television programs that she watched in her bedroom with earphones every night until she fell asleep.

"Mama, why don't you tell them if they want turkey to make it themselves?" Herminda said again, as she had the past two years. Her mother also made *empanandas* and *cazuela de mariscos,* a fish soup with potatoes, pumpkin, peppers, and corn that both she and José loved, but each year she made less.

Her mother shrugged. "We get together; that's important. Besides, I'm getting to like turkey. I just wish Ricardo had a phone."

Back to Ricardo, Herminda thought, always back to Ricardo. Sometimes she felt grateful that her father had left when she was two; she imagined her mother waiting on him for every little thing simply because he was a man. And if he was like most men and fathers she knew, her mother would probably have to bring in most of the money, just as she did now. Her uncle, Herminda considered, was responsible, but he was a cold man. He was all business; his family was business; he didn't feel warmly toward anyone, as far as she could tell.

Her mother was going on in Spanish about the neighbor's fights and how she was going to ask José to talk to them, and Herminda tuned out. She thought of Mickey, of the red hairs on the backs of his hands. She wondered if he had red chest hair. She wondered what his chest looked like.

Silvia wandered into the kitchen, blurry-eyed, and stood in front of the sink and drank a glass of water. Her face was pale. Probably trying to lubricate a hangover, Herminda thought. Her long black hair was soft and loose down her back without its usual dose of stiffening hair spray.

Herminda had heard her come in last night around 10:30. For the past year Silvia had a pattern: she stopped in at her mother's room to report that she was in and say goodnight, and then she went to her bedroom, making a big deal of closing the door.

Fifteen minutes later or so, she'd tiptoe out and let in her boyfriend, the latest one, and sneak him into her room. Her mother couldn't hear anything; she wore her earphones from 8 p.m. until midnight when she fell asleep.

But from her bedroom on the porch, Herminda could hear them: first it would be quiet, then there would be some giggling, and then the sounds became more urgent, more serious—she'd hear a moan from the boy, or a strange kind of happy swearing, and then a little cry from Silvia. Sometimes this would happen quickly; sometimes it would take a long time; it depended on whether Elena was coming home. (Elena, at 18, was engaged to an older man who had his own apartment, and she spent most of her nights there. Without specifically saying so, her mother had consented to the arrangement, since they were engaged.)

When Silvia had first started bringing the boys home this way, Herminda had been shocked. Disgusted, even. In the hallway to the bathroom, Silvia would give her a defiant look, daring her to say anything. Herminda tried to reveal nothing of her feelings of anxiety and curiosity in her look back. After a couple of times like this, seeing Herminda wasn't going to tell their mother about the bedroom encounters, Silvia relented. "I'm using birth control," she said suddenly one time when they were both in the bathroom at the same time.

"That's good," Herminda said.

Eventually, listening to the weekend routines, Herminda had grown used to the noise, numbed to it. There were at least two regular boys that she saw Silvia with. She was curious whether Silvia was really enjoying herself, or just putting on a show, imitating women she'd seen in movies. She wondered what kind of birth control she was using—pills? but what about STDs, then?—but she and Silvia had never been close, and she wasn't about to ask her younger sister those kinds of questions now.

"It's great, you know," Silvia said, just last week while moussing her hair straight up over her forehead like the other Mission girls. "Sex," she said to the mirror, as if Herminda wouldn't know from her tone of voice what she was talking about. Although she was three years older than Silvia, Herminda was smaller, and often felt younger. She grinned slyly at Herminda. "You should *try* it sometime, Meanie."

"It's not something you can just *try*," Herminda said quickly, feeling her face flush.

"Why not? You think it's just something for guys to like? I mean, if you got protection, why not enjoy yourself? You got to get something for yourself." Silvia was rouging her cheeks. She wore too much make-up; their mother was always complaining that she looked like a whore.

"You're not a lesbo, or anything, are you?" Silvia said, only half-joking, looking over her shoulder in the mirror at her sister.

Herminda turned and left the bathroom. Perhaps she *was* a lesbian; perhaps she would never make love with anyone. She wanted to move out of this house.

In the kitchen Herminda gazed at her sister's shapely, muscular brown legs under the short pink nightgown. Since she was 10 years old, Silvia had always teased Herminda about her looks, or brought them up in an argument when Herminda was winning. "Even if that's true," Silvia would say, "who'd believe anyone who looked so strange?" There was no denying Silvia was beautiful. Since she had entered adolescence, every part of Silvia seemed soft where she herself was skinny and hard, but when

Herminda took up the bassoon, she started not to care so much. After several years of examining herself in the mirror, Herminda decided that, taken separately, her features were okay, it was just together they didn't fit into any particular definition of beautiful. She wasn't so much ugly as she was an outsider; she had grown used to that status and had come to enjoy it. What would happen to her, she couldn't imagine. It was like being unable to imagine her date on Saturday with Mickey. She hadn't told anyone about her date last weekend, and she wasn't going to tell them about this weekend, either.

"So what's up?" Silvia said, pouring herself a cup of coffee now.

"Looks like you are, barely," her mother said in Spanish. Elena was the only one who spoke Spanish to her mother; the rest listened in Spanish and replied in English. Lorena Matta had given up on that, too, but refused to speak English to them, although her English was fine.

"Smells good in here," Silvia said.

Herminda pushed away from the table. "Does anyone mind if I practice a while?"

Silvia and her mother glanced at each other. Silvia shrugged. "It don't bother me. I guess I'm up for good."

"Dinner's at two." This was her mother's way of assenting. "Silvia, I want you to cut up potatoes, and call Elena. I want to see if that man of hers is coming over for dinner."

On her way to the sunporch at the back of the house, Herminda passed by Ricardo's room. The door was half open, and she peeked inside. It had been a long time since she'd been in her brother's room. A low-wattage light was on in the upper corner, making the room seem dim, like a jail cell with light from the spotlights outside sifting in. There was another lamp near the bed, but she had never seen it on. It was the same dark, cramped room as before, a narrow bed similar to her own, unmade, the sheets probably unchanged since who-knows-when; a small bookcase with an old collection of comics on the bottom shelf; a greasy ratchet set and a pipe (probably for hashish) on another. Next to the bookcase was a dresser, although it appeared that most of the clothes were on the floor in various piles. The smell of engine oil was strong in the room. No wonder he never slept here anymore, Herminda thought. She plopped herself down on the bed and wondered if Ricardo had ever brought any girls in here. In high school Clarice had been interested in Ricardo, but Herminda carefully explained that Ricardo would never go for her. Clarice was skinny like Herminda. She was on the outside, but unlike Herminda she wanted badly to be on the inside. Now she had a boyfriend and they were doing it. Herminda had wanted to tell her about Mickey but held back. She didn't want to explain anything. Whatever happened, she wanted the whole thing for herself; she didn't want to share the experience.

On the back of Ricardo's door was a poster of a naked woman with long wavy black hair, voluptuous, her lips all fat and puffy like someone had hit her, but smiling. Hispanic, Herminda noted. Ricardo kept to his own kind. Unlike herself. The thought made her get up.

In her room on the sunporch she put her horn together. For a while all three girls had shared the same room at the front of the flat, and Herminda had practiced her instrument out here. (Her mother always called the bassoon an "instrument," embarrassed by its awkwardness. "Couldn't you play the flute?" she asked. When Herminda had said there were no openings for flute in the high school band, and they needed a bassoonist, her mother shrugged. "Do what you want. You got to pay for it, though." Herminda paid for the rental, and later convinced her uncle to loan her money to buy the Fox. She kept it in its case and tried to practice when her mother wasn't around.)

Gradually she had moved all her things onto the porch, buying a piece of carpeting as insulation against the painted wood floor, and plastic and bamboo shades for all the windows. When she moved her bed out to the porch, her mother relented and bought her a space heater. It could still get quite cold in the winter, but she'd gotten used to it. Now the room was almost cozy. There were a couple of lamps, and a desk, her bed, a chair and a music stand. A wooden crate from the shop served as a nightstand. She used an old trunk for her foldable clothes and hung the rest in the hall closet.

Herminda could hear most everything going on in the house from the porch, but she'd discovered that the reverse wasn't so, or, in any case, when she was out on the porch everyone seemed to forget about her. She was still uncomfortable practicing when others were around, but it was unavoidable today. She needed to work on the Mozart duet Gerald had given her, and she just wanted the feel of the instrument, its weight, in her hands. The other night she had dreamed that the bassoon was part of her body, a strange appendage, and when she tried to talk her voice came through the instrument as music. Just odd little notes, sometimes recognizable as melody, sometimes just scrabble. In the dream she grew used to communicating this way. When she woke up Herminda felt oddly pleased, comforted by the dream, and glad to see her case across the room.

At 12:30, as she expected, her mother came to her door and told her to get Ricardo. She'd tried calling, she said, but no one was answering at Raul's.

"Why can't Silvia go?"

"She went out."

"She always goes out."

"Are you going, or not?"

"I'm going, I'm going." Herminda took her horn apart—there would be no more chances to play today—and grabbed an *empanada* to munch on her way.

Raul's was just around the corner, but she took the long way there. It was cloudy and warm, almost humid. Herminda put on her dark glasses and squinted up at the sky. The clouds were thin and would probably melt off by late afternoon. Almost every building was different from the next, some flat-roofed and covered in stucco, and some peaked-roof Victorians, most with bay windows, and all different colors: beige, and yellow, and mustard. At the end of the block was a Victorian painted bright pink with purple shutters. In the middle of the block were a couple of cheap modern buildings with flat fronts and tiny living room windows. Even most of the single-family homes had been modified slightly to accommodate more than one family.

And all the families had more than one car, which were usually parked haphazardly on the street and sidewalk like so many jammed-up dominoes, and some days it seemed like not one of the hundreds of vehicles was drivable. Even though it was a holiday, the street was busy, and guys were out working on their cars. Herminda stepped over four mounds of dog shit and three sets of grease-spotted pantlegs half under a car in the one block. Just exactly what they were doing, she didn't know. And there were eight or nine children in the street, the older ones playing football in between occasional cars trying to get by on the street, and the younger ones chasing each other up and down the block. She used to know the kids, but not anymore. These kids were wilder than she and her sisters had been. They were let out early and kept out until late. On an evening walk you could hear mothers screaming and fathers yelling; the street was never quiet until after one or two in the morning. Herminda imagined New York again. At least it never got really hot here. That kept a lid on some of the tension. Most residents were tenants; Herminda's situation, with a relative owning the building, was unusual.

Herminda's favorite building was the Victorian at the end of the block. Unlike the other houses, it had a tiny yard, accented by a white picket fence that was constantly being repainted to cover graffiti. Two white men lived there and parked their car in the tiny garage around the corner, painted the same purple and pink as the house, with a higher white fence blocking a view of the backyard. It looked like a small gingerbread house, with scalloped shingles around a small window on the second floor. One time, looking at the house, Herminda noticed a man looking out that window at her. He looked thin and sickly, and they stared at each other for about 10 seconds or so. Then he smiled at her, briefly, and turned away from the window. This morning there was a ROOM FOR RENT sign, with "Special Situation" scrawled in underneath posted in the corner of the living room window. Maybe she would tell Roland about it.

There were a couple of other white people on the block—students—but the yuppies had all moved out, to Potrero Hill or Noe Valley, or they had never moved in.

Around the corner on Alabama, someone had put several plastic dolls' heads on the spiked tops of the fence. Herminda wondered if the men from the house did it as a joke, or if someone else had put them there. It wasn't the messing-around style of anyone she knew.

Ricardo was where she had supposed him to be—under a car with Raul. She recognized his black canvas high-tops. A plastic tub filled with thick engine oil and two open cans of beer stood waiting by the jack.

"You coming to dinner today, brother?" she asked.

"Hey, Meanie," she heard from under the car. He stayed under the car for another minute. The garage door was open, revealing a mess of greasy tools and baby paraphernalia, including an aging umbrella stroller and car seat that belonged to Raul's girlfriend who didn't live with Raul anymore. The baby was three now, and Herminda had heard that she was expecting another, by someone else. For a man with a business and some respectability, José's sons hadn't turned out much better than anyone else's. Maybe worse, she thought.

Raul must have been on the roller, because Ricardo had to scrape himself out from under the car. He stood up slowly and brushed some gravel off his flannel shirt. Even though he was usually meticulous about the way he looked, Ricardo would slip under any car in any outfit. There was a streak of grime on the tail of his shirt, which he now examined as if his sister weren't standing there in front of him. She could tell by the way he stood that her brother had had more than one beer—probably several by now.

"Sure, *hermanita mia,* I'll be there. Free food. Hey, can Raul come, too?" He tapped the bottom of his cousin's sneaker with his foot, and Raul gave a grunt from underneath the car. Raul and his brother were always expected at their *abuela*'s for holidays. Herminda was grateful for this.

She heard a door slam and saw her other cousin Felix coming from the house into the garage out of the corner of her eye. She turned away abruptly. "Dinner's at two," she said, stepped over Raul's legs and turned back the way she had come.

Dinner was quiet, almost strange. Ricardo was late, and they started without him. Elena had come while Herminda was out to retrieve him and helped their mother set the table. She had to leave early to have a second dinner with Roberto's family, and kept glancing at the clock over the sink. When Ricardo arrived, he was drunk, but quietly so. He washed up at the kitchen sink. For once, no one started an argument. José arrived about the time Elena left, and he and his sister went into the living room for their brandies while Silvia and Herminda cleaned up the dishes. Ricardo had a brandy with his mother and uncle (his mother allowed him to drink with them), and then came into the kitchen.

"You still playing music, Meanie?" he asked.

"Yeah."

"Good," he said, putting his glass in the sink, not knowing what else to say.

Herminda figured he would be meeting his cousins in a bar on Mission, El Rico.

"Well, *hasta la vista*—babies," he said, and kissed both Silvia and Herminda on the cheek as he was leaving.

When José left, Lorena Matta took a shower and went into her bedroom with her headset to watch television, like any other day. Silvia went out, and Herminda sat on the front stoop until dusk. Others were doing the same, watching their children or grandchildren in the street, drinking coffee or beer. She might have called Clarice, but Clarice had a big family and she would have had to socialize with them, and then Clarice would probably want to go out with Stefan who could get her into a bar, and Herminda didn't feel like going out.

She watched the neighborhood, but she didn't feel like part of it. Even when, as a kid, Silvia would get her to join in some game, some screaming match with the others down the street, Herminda hadn't felt like it was really herself participating. She was always the watcher. Three years ago, on Thanksgiving, when Ricardo had been on his own peculiar rampage, sullen and high most of the time, he'd yelled at Herminda in Spanish, "You're just a white bitch in a scrawny brown body!" Their mother had started screaming and ordered him out of the house. Herminda had been too stung to cry. What had he been referring to, she wondered now. Her music? The way she didn't like dating, hadn't wanted to go out with any of the assholes he said he could set her up with? She couldn't remember. He was fucked up. A few weeks later they kicked him out of high school. A sympathetic counselor at the school got him into drug rehab. When he came back home a month later, he was still sullen but not high. He apologized for his outburst. "I didn't know what I was saying," he said to Herminda. "I was crazy in the head." Now, he drank, but he didn't fool around with the messier stuff. He was glad she was taking music lessons, he said. "The only one in the family with any brains, to go any place."

Sitting on the stoop, Herminda knew she would go someplace, but had no clear picture where. Playing the bassoon, even if she was good, would probably not land her a job. And even if she did find work as a musician, what else? Would someone love her? Would she get married? (She thought of Mickey, but her thoughts strayed quickly. She didn't *know* him.)

Would she stay in the city? Usually she felt excited thinking of these questions, but tonight they depressed her.

The phone rang and Herminda knew her mother would never pick it up with her headphones on so she bounded back into the kitchen to get it.

"Herminda? Gerald Poulin." It took her a second to comprehend that Gerald was calling her at home. Something must be very wrong, she thought, but his voice was normal, calm and nasal. She felt a moment of panic about the lesson she'd had to cancel yesterday.

"I trust you're having a pleasant holiday," he said.

"Yeah, fine."

"Well I was wondering if you wanted to go through some music, do some extra time tomorrow, late afternoon. No charge, of course," he added.

"Yeah, sure," she said, wishing she would stop saying "yeah" to everything. She resolved to say "yes." She wondered what was behind the free time.

"And you could come and practice here for a while, if you like—if you need the space."

"That would be good. It's been hard to get around to it at home."

"Okay. Tomorrow, at 4."

When he answered the door the next day, he was wearing a white button-down shirt with the tails out and blue jeans that were baggy and hung down in the back. Herminda felt like saying she didn't think he knew what jeans *were*, but didn't.

Gerald looked down at his pants. "This is the end of my wardrobe," he said, abashed. "All my slacks are at the cleaners."

"Your slacks."

"Slacks," he said sternly, "are more comfortable than blue jeans."

She snickered. She noticed a duffel bag by the front door but didn't see any other sign of the blonde man.

"I've set you up in the bedroom if you don't mind. I'm making dinner." They usually had their lessons in the kitchen, so Herminda was intrigued. She felt nervous. Why the free time? But she wasn't going to ask.

Gerald's bedroom was large, with a bay window looking out the same direction as the living room, toward downtown. Gerald had a chair and music stand set up perpendicular to the view. "I set up this way so I don't get distracted," he explained. "Also, the music is easier to read. There's a little light on the stand if you like." Gerald clicked on the light on the upper edge of the stand. White block letters spelled out: "SAN FRANCISCO OPERA."

She thanked him. It occurred to her that she would have to practice harder than usual if he was around. After he left, Herminda took a look around the room. There was a second door to the bathroom from the bedroom, and a large closet with folding doors. A king size bed, neatly made with a beige and brown pattern comforter, faced the view. There was a nightstand with a clock-radio, small lamp and a framed photograph of Gerald and another man who must be his boyfriend.

The boyfriend was a big man, maybe eight inches taller than Gerald, with a mustache and thick black hair mixed with gray. He looked to be about 50. In the photo the man had his arm around Gerald and they were both smiling widely as if about to break into a laugh. Herminda tentatively picked up the frame, glancing behind her in case Gerald came in. The photo must have been taken in the spring—there was that kind of clear light in the background—on the stairs in front of the flat. Herminda recognized the thick scarlet strand of bougainvillea behind them. The startling feature about the photo, though, was Gerald's bald head. There was a ridge of red hair circling his head for about an inch above his ear, and then the white, slightly freckled skin of his skull. Had he forgotten to put on the toupee, she wondered, or did the boyfriend and the person taking the photo convince him to take it off? Herminda felt a wave of surprise and affection toward Gerald for letting her come to his house, and letting her into this room where he practiced. He must have known she would look around, that she would see this picture.

She put her instrument together and took a long time warming up. She was tired, but in a way it was good; she was too tired to be distracted, and concentrated on the sound. She practiced for an hour. The sun had gone down just after she arrived, and out of the corner of her eye she could see the red and orange streaks across the bay. She turned on the small light of the music stand. Occasionally she heard Gerald puttering around in the other room. The phone rang. A smell of garlic and onions drifted into the room.

Gerald knocked on the door. "I was thinking you might want to play that duet," he said.

"The Mozart? Sure."

Gerald got his bassoon from the other room, and Herminda set up the music while he warmed up a bit. They'd only played it together once before.

"Okay, ready? On four," he said, and they began. Herminda's nerves dissolved into concentration after the first few measures and she was aware of Gerald's black-socked foot on the floor. Their feet did not tap, but the rhythm of the piece was inside them both. The end of his bassoon shook slightly. He flipped the page. Herminda's palms were sweating in anticipation of the difficult section in the middle of the next page, but she managed through it with only a few bungled notes.

"Let's switch parts," he said.

"I haven't worked on your part."

He shrugged. "Don't worry about it." He set the music up at the beginning again. "Just watch the upbeats. Concentrate only on what's in front of you. Don't listen to me. It'll be hard." As an afterthought he said, "It'll be good. For you."

"Yeah, right."

They played the piece again with reversed parts and Herminda wallowed through it. By the third time she knew the tricky spots and played passably. Light pooled out in a fan shape over the music and the darkening room surrounded them. When the piece ended, the notes seemed to hang in the air. They were both quiet. Out the window, the orange lights of Market Street curled out like a tail. Lights from houses and apartments flickered in the night air. Some people had already put up their Christmas lights, and a strand of red and blue lights blinked in the yard behind Gerald's building. Herminda had a feeling opposite of her feeling last night on the stoop, almost of peace. If Gerald were someone else, she might have touched him, taken his hand.

"This is a good room," she said quietly.

"Yes, it is," he said.

The phone rang again. He put his horn down to take the call in the other room.

"I think I'm through," Herminda said to him, standing up. "I'll just get my stuff together."

In the living room Gerald put his hand up to halt her for a moment. The jeans hung down in the back almost past his heels and every half minute or so he hitched them up. Herminda wondered whether they belonged to his boyfriend.

He hung up. "John can't make it." He looked at her and shrugged. "Would you like to join me for dinner, Herminda? There's quite a lot of food."

For a second she wondered whether Gerald had staged all this. "Are you sure? I feel like I've barged in already."

"Well," he said, "You haven't. It'll be ready in two minutes. You know where the washroom is," he said, like a father, and went back into the kitchen.

Chapter 7

He had made chicken and vegetables over rice with some stir-fry sauce he bought at a Chinese grocery. John had first taken him to the small shop just outside Chinatown. The man at the grocery didn't speak English, but now he knew Gerald when he came in and always got him the sauce and some special dried mushrooms and miso. Gerald had been hoping John would come by for dinner, but some old friends from John's "married life" had come into town unexpectedly and Gerald didn't feel like going out with them. Also, Herminda was here, and he didn't want to rush her; in fact, he'd asked her over with the intention of talking about the spring concert.

"Sorry I couldn't...." Herminda murmured something he didn't catch.

"What?"

"I said, I'm sorry I missed the other day. My uncle needed me to stay late." She eyed him. Even her apologies were defensive.

He shrugged. Perhaps she thought he was emotionally involved in whether she took lessons, but continuing on the bassoon was up to her. Berkowski wanted to do *Rite of Spring* in May, and Gerald wanted Herminda on second bassoon. He was going to talk to her about it, but now he felt hesitant. If he didn't get this constant feeling of defensiveness from her, it would be easier.

Sometimes he thought Herminda did not know she was talented. He wouldn't work with her if he didn't believe in her talent. She was probably a better sight reader than he was, and when she was concentrating she had a lovely tone. He had enjoyed doing the Mozart with her a little while ago in his room. But being a musician was so much more than talent; it was temperament, timing, luck. Patience. He had thought of talking to her about practicing more, maybe taking more lessons. Her home life must be chaotic, he speculated, remembering the noise in the background on the two occasions he'd called. And what had she said about her room being cold? Perhaps she could practice here, like today—work out a schedule. But what would be accomplished by that? He had nothing to offer her. There was nothing available out there now, nothing that would give a salary. Herminda had no special training, no degree, and no connections in that world. He watched her pack up her horn. She was wearing a large gray tee-shirt with SHA-ZAMM! printed on it diagonally in red and silver letters, baggy jeans, and the familiar red canvas hightops. What image did she have of herself? Her clothes, with that long, shaggy haircut, made her appear both anonymous and strange looking to him. Gerald sighed, and she turned from gazing out the window, smiling hesitantly at him.

The present tense. What table settings should he use? When he ate in, he liked to have settings. There was pleasure in that order, in the time taken for it, the color of the plates on the mats, the clarity of the wine glasses, the food on the plate. Even when he was home alone, Gerald liked to lay out a setting. It was a ritual: put on some music, turn down the lights, and eat in front of the sliding glass door.

The rust mats and the black plates, he decided.

"How was your Thanksgiving?" Herminda asked.

"What?" he said loudly, startled by her sudden effort at conversation.

"Your Thanksgiving, how was it?"

"Oh, uneventful. Neither of us felt like cooking, so John and I went out." Roland had said he was going to visit "friends" in the East Bay until tomorrow, which was, Gerald thought, a rare move of consideration. John and he had gone to a new place in the Castro, and the food had been bad, another tip from one of John's unreliable co-workers. Roland's name had come up several times during dinner. "I don't see why you're letting him stay with you. Obviously he has *friends* somewhere, if he's off for a couple of days."

"John," Gerald said, trying to joke, "are you jealous?"

John's face reddened. "*Should* I be? Really. I don't think so."

They'd both been out of sync and irritable, and John left him at the door. But he'd come by this morning and things had evened out again.

"John—that's the guy in the photo in your room?" Herminda asked.

"That's the guy," Gerald handed her the bottle of wine and two glasses. "Do you drink wine?"

Herminda blinked. "Yeah, sure."

He poured a glass for her. "So, John. I've known him for six years now. He's a year older than me—52—he's a real estate agent and has been for 25 years. He was married for a while, has one grown son. I met him in a produce shop in the Mission."

"No kidding. Which one?"

"21st and...Mission."

"No kidding!" she exclaimed again. "That's my uncle's place, where I work." Herminda seemed genuinely delighted at this discovery. Her face changed, became more symmetrical somehow. She became... attractive, Gerald noted with surprise.

"Well, I wondered about that. I'll tell John. He still goes there a lot."

"Do you?"

"Sometimes." Gerald poured a glass of wine for himself and pulled a chair out for her to sit down.

"Why don't you live together?" This was a bold question for her.

Gerald dished out some rice and the chicken with vegetables, thinking of last night. Before he left John had said, "Gerald, I can see why you don't live with anyone." He'd said this before, many times, and now he said it again, quietly. He could easily have said, *I can see why no one will live with you.* Gerald no longer knew whether he appreciated this tact.

"We like our space," he said to Herminda.

"Yeah," she said, nodding as though she wished for some privacy of her own.

They looked out the window for a few moments. The wine was dry, he noted, and just right for the meal. Herminda held her fork like a handle.

"This tastes good," she said. "It's a nice view."

"So what about you, Herminda? Seeing anyone?"

She blushed and struggled to finish the food that was in her mouth. It was only a casual question, really, but Gerald almost wished he hadn't asked. He had never imagined Herminda with anyone; she seemed so young, for one thing. Who would she date? He couldn't picture her with any men her own age, Latin or otherwise; they wouldn't be able to take her determination. He couldn't imagine Herminda sexually, but then he found it difficult imagining women sexually at all.

"No one. Really," Herminda answered, finally, as if trying to decide. She was clutching and unclutching the stem of her wine glass.

The "really" made Gerald smile. So she *was* seeing someone.

"And Thanksgiving? Did you have a big gathering?"

She shook her head. "No. Just my mom and my sisters. My brother came by later. My uncle, too. Mom pretends she doesn't care that she's not invited to his family's. But she wishes she was." She shrugged. "But, anyhow, nobody got into a fight. It was kind of quiet." She paused. "I was glad when you called. I wished I could have had a lesson last week." She glanced at him quickly, then looked again to the view.

"I saw your friend Roland," she said, her eyes darting to the duffel bag by the front door.

"Oh?"

"He comes into the cafe almost every day. He's looking for a place. He has the want ads with him. I actually heard of a place, if he doesn't mind being in the Mission."

"Well, I'll tell him. He'll be back tomorrow." Gerald pushed away from the table to make coffee.

"Did you say he was your cousin?"

"He's my aunt's grandson. My father's sister's daughter's son." He smirked. "That's what I tell people. My second cousin. I first met him about six years ago."

"Oh."

Gerald felt the weight of questions in her response, and it occurred to him that Roland might have some plan in his head, stopping at the café where Herminda worked. Maybe Roland intended to tell her about when he first stayed here. It wouldn't surprise him. What would she think? Would she be disgusted? It would be a boundary crossed over, like inviting her to dinner. He almost felt like telling her, right now.

"You kind of act like you don't like him," she said.

"I do?"

Herminda shrugged.

"I like Roland fine. It's just that things can be...*he* can be difficult."

The coffee was ready. Gerald's palms stuck to the coffee mugs, and he had to dry them with a towel.

"Listen," he said suddenly to Herminda. "Let's have our coffee in the living room. I want you to hear something." They took their mugs to the couch and Gerald put on the CD of the Boston Symphony. "Berkowski wants to play *The Rite of Spring* for the last performance this season, in May. You know the piece, right?"

Herminda nodded, frowning.

"Well," he didn't want to say anything else too suddenly. "Just listen to it."

Gerald had only performed *Le Sacre du Pritemps* twice—shortly after he joined the Symphony, and again seven years ago. There was a ballet that went with it, but it was conceived later, after the music, and he had only seen the ballet performed once. The dancers represented the spring ritual of an ancient tribe, rejoicing that spring was coming and choosing a young girl to be a sacrifice to the earth, an offering to ensure the tribe's survival.

When the ballet was first performed in Paris in 1913, the outraged audience stopped the performance midway. Gerald speculated that it was just too much for them then—the strange ballet, the chord blots, dissonance and polytonality.

Seventy years later, when he saw it, Gerald had found the ballet distracting. On its own, though, the music was complex, bizarrely focused. He remembered being almost frightened the first time he performed it, twenty years ago—the violence of the sounds pulsating from the percussion and then the strings. As a musician, it was like being washed in an ocean, entirely rhythmic but unpredictable, time changing measure to measure from 2/4 to 5/4 to 7/4 to 5/8—you were caught up, perturbed, excited.

Now, he knew just how the conductor would tick off a measure or two before the bassoon came in: that short, lovely solo that still made him feel like something was opening up inside him, that made the hairs on his forearms stand up. Just a simple solo. Not that much to it. He glanced over at Herminda; there was a small smile on her face, like pleasure. He was glad she wasn't looking at him, glad she wasn't attempting to respond to his response, as Richard always did when Gerald played him something.

They listened in silence to the first two sections. Then Gerald clicked off the CD player and turned to Herminda. "Would you like to play second bassoon on this?"

"How?" she asked warily.

"Would you *like* to?"

"Of course. Definitely." She was biting her bottom lip.

"Cynthia Houseworth is due to have her baby a week before the concert; she's requested a leave. I was telling this to Berkowski, but the program's been set; I know he wants to do it, and if we get regulations straight with the union I don't think there'll be a problem."

"What about the third bassoonist?"

"I think I'll ask Richard to play third. And Leonard—you don't know him— will play fourth."

"*Fourth?*"

"Four bassoons, yes." Gerald smiled. Stravinsky liked his woodwinds. "Leonard won't mind. He just goes about his business. Besides, he'll also be on contra-bassoon for this."

"It'd be so...strange," she said.

"What do you mean?"

"I don't know. Just...strange, playing with a symphony—a real one—not a high school thing."

"Well, you need to. And I think you can do it. We'll work on it. You have to be ready to play that opening solo, too."

He saw the expression on her face and shrugged. "You never know. I've had to fill in many times for first bassoonists. They get sick; their reed cracks at the last minute...you have to be ready."

She was clenching her coffee mug.

"You'll have to make the rehearsals, too. There'll only be four or five of them, but they'll be in the morning."

Herminda nodded.

"Of course, all this is a ways away. It's only December. Rehearsals won't start until April."

She nodded again.

"So, what do you think?"

"I think...*great!*" she said, standing up suddenly. "It's great." Once up, Herminda didn't seem to know what to do. She put her hands in her pockets, glanced around without looking directly at him, then took them out of her pockets. She went over to the table and started clearing the dishes. "It's great," he heard her say again, and he let her clear the table.

"Do you want to hear the rest of it?" he asked when she had finished.

"Sure."

Gerald poured himself a glass of brandy and dimmed the lights. Everyone incorporated music, he thought. Everyone used it to mark time—a first meeting, a time in one's life, a death. As a musician he had more music to live through. It was always around him—in restaurants, at stop lights in his car—infiltrating, making a place, settling around all the talk of regular people's lives—of people who weren't musicians.

He wondered whether *Rite* would mark Stephen's death. He didn't want any markings. He wanted Stephen around so long there was no particular piece that would remind Gerald of him.

He began the CD again. Finally, after the opening, and past the first section where the clarinets and oboe came in, he stopped seeing the score in his mind; he stopped thinking about Stephen, and Roland. He looked over at Herminda, absorbed in the music, which was loud and jarring—not music to muse upon—and he knew he was lying to himself about not caring whether she played or not. She saw him looking at her and smiled. He wanted her to play, to give herself over to the instrument, to the music. He wanted her, just then, to be like him.

He was embarrassed by this and looked away. And after the piece ended and they had finished their coffee, when the silence became uncomfortable, Herminda said her thanks, took her instrument and left, and Gerald sat back down on the couch with another glass of brandy, looking out the window until John came over, a little while later.

Chapter 8

The bartender at El Rio was good friends with Mickey and gave Herminda only a glance of friendly curiosity as he passed her the beer Mickey had ordered for her. The only times she had been in a bar before were to retrieve her brother or pass along to him some message from their mother. She would be 21 next month, but Mickey had teased her, "Minda, you'll be *41* before they stop carding you."

She adjusted herself carefully on the barstool and looked around. Just a few days from Christmas, the bar was decked out with streamers of tiny red and green lights crisscrossing the ceiling and two fake Christmas trees blinking on and off in the corners. As if in competition, several Stars of David dangled in both rooms of the bar, twirling with the draft of the ceiling fans and flashing so that from the corner of her eye it looked like flashbulbs were going off. It was early, about 6, and the crowd was mixed— a couple of women (gay, she suspected from their flannel shirts, crewcuts and multiple dangling earrings) shooting pool, two or three regulars at the bar (all of them looked like they were in their late thirties), and a man and woman sitting by the doors to the patio holding hands. Herminda recognized the song on the jukebox by Mercedes Sosa and felt very strange to be hearing that sad, lyrical love song in this bar. Her palms tingled. She took another gulp of the Mexican beer.

She watched Mickey put his hand through his hair, which looked almost bleached in the barroom light. He wore a long sleeve shirt with cuffs rolled up to the middle of his forearms, maroon with blue stripes. Herminca liked the way his forearms looked—capable, muscular, and yet tentative. She liked the way he didn't wear a belt with his jeans; she didn't know why. The beer tasted good. The very things about Mickey that she had thought were too collegiate four weeks ago when they'd first gone to the movies were now attractive.

Mickey was talking to the bartender, whose name was Jay, but when he caught her looking at him he stopped and smiled at her and took her hand. The bartender, cut off mid-sentence, raised his eyebrows at her as if to comment on her unusual power over his friend. Herminda didn't know how to look back, and instead looked at Mickey's hand on hers. He stroked each finger lightly, one by one, as if fascinated. Now, instead of a tingling in her palms, she felt a tingling in her stomach.

Each time they'd gone out, except for that first time, they had parted with a light kiss. The first time Mickey kissed her, she froze as his face approached her, her eyes open as he touched his lips to hers and pulled back. The next time she anticipated, and kissed back, her eyes still open. She liked how his skin, so white, was smooth except for the crinkles around his eyes—not big-pored, like some white men. After that kiss, she approached him a few times and they kissed longer—once on the street, and he'd put his hand on her hip. She liked that.

Somewhere in the back of her mind perhaps she'd thought she would never make love, and now here was this man who was interested in her. She watched his fingers on hers and felt a tightening in her stomach again. If she had been bolder, or had a few more beers, she would have asked him bluntly: Are we going to do it? Are we? And then what?

"You ready?" Mickey asked, tilting his head toward the door. The plan was to go to his place for the first time, and meet his son Christopher, and have dinner.

"I don't cook much at home," he was saying as they walked to his car. "I usually just bring stuff home from the restaurant. But for *you*, well...." He got into the car and unlocked her side.

Herminda had never asked Mickey exactly where he lived, which was near but not quite in Bernal Heights. She had imagined his place several times. Each time she imagined it differently—sometimes it was high-ceilinged and open; other times it was cozy and dark, but why had she never asked him where he lived. She could have walked to his place from her house.

"I've got the driveway in exchange for taking the bottom flat," Mickey was saying as he pulled into the narrow drive which consisted of two concrete trails with grass growing between. They got out and he led her up a few haphazard wooden stairs in need of paint. "But that's okay, because if we were in the upper one, Christopher would drive the other tenants crazy with his thumping." Mickey smiled at her and made his fingers run back and forth in the air like an imaginary Christopher and unlocked first the bolt and then the door.

For the moment Herminda had forgotten Mickey's son.

That was impossible to do once the door was open: there was evidence of a child everywhere—a tiny bike with training wheels against the hallway wall, five or six green plastic figures on the floor, and a long sheet of butcher paper taped along the length of the hallway with all kinds of drawings on it. She could make out a long beach and sun and, further down, some race cars on a track.

Mickey caught her looking. "After having to paint the walls once, I figured this was easier," he said under his breath, then called out, "Who's home?"

"*Dad!*" came the exclamation and the sound of chairs scooting, and then a smaller image of Mickey—lanky, with red hair—appeared in the kitchen doorway, dressed in blue polyester pajamas, a half-eaten hot dog in his hand. He appeared to be about 4 or 5 years old.

"Christopher! How are you." Mickey knelt down and gave him a hug.

"Are you going away again?" the child said, looking suspiciously at Herminda.

"No, I'm here. Why?"

"Is that the other babysitter?" he asked, pointing at her.

"No, no, no," Mickey said, scooping Christopher up, and bringing him over closer to Herminda. "This is a friend of mine, Herminda. She's come for dinner."

She smiled hesitantly at Mickey's son. "Hi, Christopher."

"She looks like Gabrielle," Christopher said, blinking at her, and when the babysitter came around the corner Herminda understood why. She was also Hispanic, thin, and possibly only a couple of years younger than Herminda—it was hard to tell. "I made the salad like you said, Mickey," she was saying, drying her hands. She stopped when she saw Herminda and they both looked at each other warily.

"Gabrielle, this is a friend of mine—Herminda," Mickey said, a little loudly.

Herminda put out her hand and the babysitter took it limply.

Mickey walked Gabrielle to the front door and pulled out several bills from his wallet. "She lives upstairs," he said after the door was closed.

"Oh."

"C'mon," he said, taking her hand, "let's get something to eat. The pasta will only take a few minutes."

Good thing you got your girl to make the salad, Herminda thought, feeling suddenly mean.

In the kitchen there were two chairs by the small wooden table pushed up against the wall, one with a red plastic booster seat. Mickey removed the booster and she sat down. He poured her a glass of wine from an open bottle in the refrigerator. Christopher had brought a small truck into the kitchen and was driving it in and out of the black and white squares of the linoleum, and for a few minutes she watched Mickey chop garlic and talk to his son as if she wasn't there. It was familiar, watching him move around the kitchen, just like at the café. The only thing strange was realizing this was his own place.

"Whaddaya say, buddy," Mickey said, scooping up Christopher from the floor. "Let's read a book and hit the sack."

"Let's read a book and hit the sack," Christopher imitated, smacking his lips. There was none of the anxiety of half an hour ago on his face.

"Say goodnight to Herminda."

"G'night Meandah."

She smiled at him. "Goodnight."

"You don't mind?" Mickey said. "Just stir the sauce a little, would you, and I'll be back in a flash."

Herminda nodded and got up to stir the sauce, which was olive oil, basil and chopped garlic. She felt better being allowed this space in his kitchen where she didn't have to talk or respond and could just look around, and her mean mood passed. Or maybe it was the wine.

Mickey's kitchen was orderly in the same way the kitchen at work was: pots hung from a bar mounted between the cupboards by the window; the stove and counter clean. She put the salad in the refrigerator, which didn't have a lot of food in it, but was clean. She looked through the cabinets, taking care to close each door very quietly. Cereal and flour. Peanut butter and tamari sauce. A loaf of whole wheat bread. Eight plates and five bowls. Four wine glasses (including the two they were using). Saran wrap and foil in a drawer. A toaster, cappuccino maker, and small food processor lined up at the end of the long counter. The room reminded her of Gerald's kitchen. In fact, in surface ways the two of them were a lot alike, she thought. How strange it was that the two men she knew right now would both be fastidious. Gerald was gay, of course, but still.

She would've liked to go down the dark hall and look at the other rooms, but it would be too obvious that she was exploring.

It was half an hour before Mickey finished putting Christopher to bed. She heard the muffled voices back and forth, and heard Mickey say good night several times before the door finally closed and Mickey tip-toed up the creaky hallway back to the kitchen.

"Sorry it took so long."

"That's okay. I turned the sauce off but didn't put the noodles on."

He winced. He was always trying to get her to say *pasta* rather than *noodles* at the restaurant.

"Pasta. Pasta, pasta, *pasta*," she said.

Mickey poured them both more wine without asking and stood in front of the stove until the pasta was done. She watched him drain it, scoop it into a bowl, then mix in the sauce. He was casual and efficient, just like at the restaurant.

She had meant to set the table but wasn't sure what he would want. Now he pulled out two of the eight plates and laid them on the table, two cloth napkins from the only drawer she hadn't opened, two forks and two knives, two blue candles in small glass holders from on top of the refrigerator. He scooped pasta onto her plate—much more than she could eat—then onto his own and put the salad alongside.

"Dinner is served. Finally." He smiled, lifting his glass to her.

Herminda lifted hers back and drank.

He scooted back from the table and came around to her, cupped his hand around her chin, and kissed her. It was a long kiss and grew wider and more hungry. His tongue felt large in her mouth and she could taste the wine. What did her mouth feel like to him, she wondered? How small it must seem. Between her legs now she felt so tight it was almost an ache. He probably expected they were going to do it, and she didn't know if she could. Follow through. She felt her body break out in a sweat.

Mickey didn't seem to notice. He pulled back gently from her, his eyes still closed. Then he opened them and scanned her face.

If her fear was showing, he didn't notice.

"I'm not that hungry for dinner," he said.

"No," she said.

"Are you?"

"No," she said.

"I can put the salad back in the fridge." He took her hand. "Shall we go into the other room?"

Although she felt like one, Herminda was not a virgin, technically, and she had protected herself from wondering about it for the past five years by repeating to herself that she was *not* a virgin; she knew what sex was.

It had happened on a Saturday, five years ago when she was 15. She was alone in the apartment; her cousin Felix was high on something and looking for her brother. She told him he could wait. She was cleaning up, and then she was going to practice. Her bassoon was set up in her room on the sunporch, and Felix had laughed when he saw it. "Looks like a humungous prick," he'd said in Spanish. "How does a little girl like you get it on with such a big prick?" He'd snickered again at his joke and Herminda ignored him.

Felix had followed her as she went from her room to her sisters' room, changing sheets and putting dirty clothes in piles, one of many chores her mother had mandated since they were children. (She stayed out of Ricardo's room, which was more like a dark closet, filled with junk and small piles of clothes.) It was only since he entered high school that Felix had started using crack and turned into a jerk. She figured it was Felix's stepfather who started it. He was a big man who slapped him around and belittled him when he was home for being out on the streets, so Felix stayed out more and more. More than one time Felix had arrived sniffling with a bloody nose or a bruised face, and she could hear Ricardo out on the porch with him talking him down, telling him he should leave and get his own place. This was useless advice, she knew, since Felix had not finished high school and had no particular skills. There were only a couple of things he could do to make the kind of money he would need to move out. But they didn't talk about that. After a while they would both come in and Felix would stay on the couch for a couple of nights. Herminda was used to Felix; they'd grown up together.

So she was surprised when he reached out and put his hand on her shoulder from behind. It was a tentative touch, then rough. They were in her mother's room. She was bending over to change the sheet, and he pushed her down suddenly on the bed. He was small, but she was smaller. He flipped her over on the bed and put his forearm against her throat. "Felix!" she screamed once, and then he put his hand over her mouth. She heard the rip of the zipper on her jeans. She tried to move her lower body, but he pressed his knee against her thigh and held her to the bed.

"You're so scrawny," he said. His voice was soft. At another time it might have been something he would have said with affection. He didn't look at her; his face was turned to the side. She could see beads of sweat along his hairline.

He put his hand against her crotch to feel her. "You're wet!" he exclaimed, almost gleeful.

If he hadn't had his hand over her mouth, she would have told him she was having her period; that what he was feeling was blood, and maybe it would gross him out. She tried to yell, but he clamped his hand tighter. And then there was a strange pressure, and a sharp pain, and then not much feeling at all—just wetness. She thought of her mother's white bedspread beneath them and the mess that was being made. Felix jerked up and down on her, his hand on her thigh, breathing heavily. She had breathed heavily, too, gasping for air, trying to keep her nostrils free from the side of his palm. His hand tasted awful, like car grease and some other, bitter taste.

Then he stopped, and practically jumped off the bed, pulling up his pants in one motion, backing away toward the door of her mother's bedroom. For a second, Herminda had a vision of what she must look like from there: sprawled on the bed, her jeans and panties (sanitary pad still attached) tangled at her ankles, blood on her abdomen and thighs. His head jerked violently to one side, as though shocked at what he had done, as though someone had grabbed him from behind. "Tell...tell Ricardo I was looking for him," he sputtered ridiculously, and ran out of the house.

A scream filled her, like vomit coming all the way up through her body, but no sound came out. She was quiet. Her cheeks were wet. She felt tied to the bed. As she lay there on her back she felt like all the blood in her body was spilling out. After the menstrual blood was gone, all the rest of it would come out and just keep coming and coming until the floor was inch-deep, and she was just a flat piece of skin on her mother's bed.

From the radio in the other room—her room—she heard Vivaldi playing. The fall piece. She didn't want to hear music, but it came down the hallway anyway. It came down the hall to get her, to soothe her, and she let it come in. After a few minutes she sat up, untwisting her pants, and pulled them up. In the bathroom she opened the medicine chest quickly so she wouldn't have to see her reflection and examined herself quickly. Her legs were sore and shaky, bruises were rising on hips; her throat was sore where he had shoved his forearm, but her crotch wasn't ripped apart as she feared. She felt almost normal. The blood must have saved her, she thought, must have kept her from being hurt inside. And since it was her period, she thought, he probably couldn't get her pregnant.

She ran the bath and closed her eyes against the blood as she washed herself. *Wash, wash, wash*, she droned in a low murmur.

Then there was a high shriek from the other room, and she almost slipped trying to get out of the tub. It was her mother, who must have come home and gone to her room. Herminda had completely forgotten about the mess.

She heard her mother's footsteps running down the hall.

"Mama!" Herminda yelled, grabbing her mother's robe from the back of the bathroom door. "Mama!"

They ran into each other in the hall, bumping heads. "What about Elena, and Silvia? Are they okay?" she yelled, flinging open the door to her sisters' room.

"They're fine, Mama; they're not here. We're okay. It's okay. I will clean up the mess."

"What is going on? What is going on?" Her mother's eyes were wide and suspicious, looking at her daughter.

"Come into the kitchen," Herminda said, and sat down carefully on a kitchen chair. If she had had more time she might have been able to clean up and make up some story, but she was tired and told her mother about Felix and what had happened.

"All the blood..." her mother said, bewildered.

"I'm in my period," Herminda said, embarrassed, and looked away. She coughed to keep back a sob.

"Oh, *baby*," her mother exclaimed, and came around the table to her, holding her against her own small frame, and they both cried for a few minutes. It had been years since she had held her that way, and Herminda let herself be comforted.

"He will never enter my house again," her mother said, firmly. "*Never*. If he does, I will tell both his father and José and that will take care of him. Yes."

Then she knelt down in front of Herminda. "But you're okay, no? And you're probably safe because of your period. No one has to know. We must forget about it; we must go on like it never happened."

Herminda said nothing, gazing at her mother's tired face. She looked twenty years older than 35. Lorena Matta put her face down in her daughter's lap and cried. Herminda could smell her mother's cigarettes as she stroked the dark hair streaked with gray. Then abruptly, she had stopped crying and stood up, wiping her face with the back of her hand. She shrugged. "It happens to every woman sometime. So. Perhaps we can be glad it's over." She examined her nails, which were chipped and needed painting. "And there will be no surprises for you." She looked at the floor. "Oh, *mijita*, you're bleeding."

Her mother was all business now, and helped Herminda to the bathroom, taking the stained robe from her. "I will clean it up. You don't need to see any of that," her mother said. "Who needs a white bedspread anyway? It collects the dirt. You get cleaned up, take a nap."

After she had bathed, Herminda lay down on her bed in the sunporch. At least, she thought, it hadn't happened in here. Her room, her bed, was preserved. She looked at her horn, assembled and ready to practice on the chair by the bed. She could hear her mother in the kitchen, singing louder than normal, fiddling with the trash, probably disposing of the bedspread. Later she would take the sheets and the other piles of clothes Herminda had collected to the laundromat. She would ask Herminda whether she needed anything at the grocery. They would smile politely at each other. The rattling of the plastic on the windows of the porch muffled other noise, made the outside world opaque. The radio was still on, but instead of classical music there was a pledge drive. Her mother was right; she would have to just forget it. Herminda thought of a little exercise she had memorized from the book the orchestra leader had gotten for her to encourage her to keep working. Her hands moved automatically into the fingerings of the piece and Herminda had waited for her mother to leave so she could practice.

Except for the iron bars outside the bay windows, Mickey's living room was cozy. There was a big brown couch with a lamp next to it and two club chairs and a worn oriental rug in the middle. A television was in the corner by the window, with a sleeping bag and two oversized pillows on the floor in front of it. A built-in bookcase was adjacent to a fireplace with a mantel with several pictures of Christopher on it. She noticed a photo with a blonde woman who must be Christopher's mother.

Mickey let down the shades. "I like this room," he was saying. "Sometimes I just grab my quilt and sleep in here." Herminda remained standing in the doorway. He turned off the overhead light and then there was only a soft yellow glow from the pole lamp. Mickey paused and stood very close in front of her. Herminda could feel his breath on the top of her head. "You know," he said quietly, "when Christopher goes down, he really goes down. He won't wake up til 7 tomorrow morning." He must have thought she was hesitant because of Christopher. He put his arms around her, but she wriggled free.

"I need to talk."

Even in the low light she could see Mickey's face fall, just a little. "Sure," he said.

"I need to talk," she said again.

He took her hand and led her over to the couch and they sat down, side by side. After a few seconds, Mickey pulled his legs up and sat cross-legged.

"So," he said.

She couldn't bring herself to look at him. He was so large beside her. She had the feeling, suddenly, that he might be angry if she didn't have sex with him. And what? Hurt her? No, she was just afraid he would be angry, and then it would be over. They wouldn't see each other anymore except for awkward exchanges at the cafe.

"What, Herminda? Just say what it is." There was a resignation in his voice.

"I'm afraid," she said. It sounded so simple. She tried to make a laugh come out, but it sounded like she was about to cough.

"Is this...your first time?" he asked.

"*No*," she said abruptly.

"You're not a virgin."

"No."

"Are you afraid of *me*?"

"No," she said quickly, and looked at him for the first time and looked away. "No," she repeated. "I guess I'm afraid you'll be angry if I don't."

He shrugged. "Not angry, just....I was thinking... I thought you..." He seemed embarrassed. "What do you want, Herminda?"

"I *do*. Want it. I think."

"Want what?"

"Want you to touch me," she said very quietly. She thought she might cry. He could use her desire against her; he had it all to use against her.

Mickey uncrossed his legs and pulled her to him and put his arms around her from behind. "I had the horrible feeling you were about to say you just wanted to be friends," he said, gruffly.

They sat together quietly for a few minutes.

"So it was a bad experience?" Mickey said, finally.

"Yeah, I guess."

He waited. She examined the red hairs on the backs of his hands. "It was my cousin," she said, "Felix. He came in and did it to me. I was cleaning up the apartment. He said he was looking for Ricardo, and then he did it to me, on my mother's bed. That's it. That's all."

"Are you okay—I mean, *were* you okay?"

Herminda pulled away from him. "He didn't, like, *damage* anything." She glared at him. "I was having my period."

She could feel how he wanted to take his eyes off her but was forcing himself to meet her glare. Finally, he broke and looked down at his hands. "We don't have to make love, Herminda. We don't have to do anything. We can do whatever you want." He looked at her, and now his face seemed all soft and tired, and she wanted to kiss him. *We can do whatever you want.* She wondered whether she could believe that.

She moved toward him on her knees on the couch and kissed his forehead, then kissed him down both sides of his face, then his mouth, lightly, then harder. Mickey's mouth responded, but lightly, and he didn't move his hands from his lap. She buried her head in his shoulder and kissed his neck, smelling him, how he smelled like garlic and something sweeter—maybe Christopher—maybe soap —it couldn't be sweat—no one's sweat smelled like that—and she put her hands in his hair, and her fingers along the sworls of his ears, the roughness of his cheek, and found his mouth again. Still, Mickey kept his hands on his legs, letting her do whatever she wanted. She put a hand on his chest, but she was afraid to move further. She liked his mouth, his full lips, and the longer she kissed his mouth the more it felt like it was hers.

"Can I move my hands?" he asked and they both glanced down at his hands on his thighs. She wondered if he was hard under his jeans, what that would feel like, if it would hurt, if he would become someone she no longer knew.

"Okay."

And he put his hand on her face and stroked her cheek as they kissed. It seemed like they were kissing forever; her mouth was getting sore; and then he kissed her neck, leaning over her, kissing her down her blouse, and just stopping before her breasts, until she wanted to grab him and push him onto her breasts, and then his hand was there, out of nowhere, moving lightly across her nipples on top of the blouse and tee-shirt she was wearing. He was unbuttoning her blouse. Would he think they were too small, would he think they were like nothing, she wondered, but almost didn't care, just wanting him to kiss her there....

And then they both stopped. He helped her off with her tee-shirt, and she had to resist wrapping her arms around herself. He was going to see her, to *see* her, and then he took his shirt off, and took her hand and led her off the couch and pulled her to him standing, embracing her, his skin against hers, her face in his chest and still that smell, of a child, or maybe it was the laundry detergent he used—she wondered if he did his own washing— and he was running his hands up and down her back, pressing her to him Along her hip he could feel the hardness in his jeans, she could feel it, and wanted to, but didn't want to see it.

Mickey was leaning down to kiss her, and bending down, and then moved slowly down her body and his mouth was on her breast. Her breath came very tight and short. She hoped she wasn't gasping. He was pressing his face into her stomach, licked her navel. She could feel his hands tugging at the button on top of her jeans. He looked up at her, as if for permission, but she couldn't look at him, and she let him pull down her pants and helped her step out of them. Then he pulled down her underwear and she was naked.

"Oh," he said, looking at her as if she startled him.

"Oh," she said back, and he grinned at her, and put his face in her belly, kissing her up one hip and down the other, his hands running up and down her legs until she thought she would swoon.

"Are you warm enough?" he said, and pulled her over to the couch and wrapped them both in a blanket, leaning over her again —she liked the weight of him now, the leaning on her, kissing her mouth again, and down her body, pausing at her crotch, and then she felt his tongue on her and she jerked. He calmed her with his hands, stroking her thighs, and tried again, and she wasn't so jumpy. "You're sweet," he said, "sweet." He repeated *sweet* over and again, licking her, and his fingers were on her nipples, and it was warm under the blanket, and he wasn't going to prod her or hurt her, not now, and she began to think she was losing her breath, she felt a noise coming up through her, and then she was moving back and forth; her hands were in his hair; she wanted this to go on and on; and then, it was gone; she felt all untied, and she had the feeling of being both empty and full at the same time, the way she felt sometimes while practicing, but here with her whole body. Herminda could feel Mickey's head on her stomach, his breath warm across her skin, but she knew he was awake. She combed her fingers through Mickey's hair. Gradually, she opened her eyes, saw her hand curled in the red shock of hair and knew for a second that they were at the beginning of something, although she didn't know exactly what, or where it would take them.

Chapter 9

The Cafe Del Sol made Gerald feel like he was back in college, with its clientele of mostly students dressed in black from City College and San Francisco State, and its wood-lined walls, slightly greasy and scratched, like the walls in a sauna. It wasn't his idea to come here; Roland had left a message on the answering machine to meet him at the café for coffee after Stephen's appointment. Roland had moved out just after Thanksgiving into a house with three other young men, and Gerald had only seen him a couple of times. Apparently that hadn't worked out and now he was staying with his new boyfriend. "Bring Stephen, too," he'd said, and Gerald was impressed that Roland remembered that every other Wednesday was Stephen's day at the hospital.

"Sounds good to me. I haven't seen the R-Man for a while," Stephen had said, making a notation in a small spiral-bound notebook, and then slipping the notebook into his backpack. There was nothing new, either good or bad, to report from his appointment. He was holding steady. He kept notes on the progression of his disease—his "number" book, he called it—and lately he'd started taking down numbers from his friends who had AIDS. To Gerald, this record-keeping seemed just barely on the edge of a very dark-humored joke, but he made no comments.

He hadn't been in the café before, although he'd been by it several times since he knew Herminda worked there. He and Stephen were early and took a table by the wall. Gerald pulled the table out from under a bookcase that looked like it might fall any moment.

"I used to come in here when it was something else," Stephen was saying, looking around. "It was still a coffee house, but they didn't serve anything besides dessert."

"Herminda works here. But I don't see her today," Gerald said. He felt slightly relieved. He was uncomfortable with the idea of meeting her in a place outside of his kitchen. Gertz made positive comments about her participation in *Man of La Mancha*, but Herminda had said nothing to Gerald about playing in the musical. She'd changed in the past month; her bangs had grown out, and she'd gotten the rest of her hair cut in a bob to just below her chin. The cut improved her looks by far, making her look older.

Stephen glanced toward the kitchen. "So what's the occasion? You haven't seen Roland for a while. Why's he calling you?"

Gerald shrugged. "Your guess is probably better than mine."

At that moment they could both see Roland and a tall man with dark longish hair just outside the cafe. He must be the one Roland had been staying with, Gerald thought, a salesman at a clothing store in the Embarcadero. Tim was 42, and although on the phone Roland had gone on about how an older man was good for him, etcetera, and Gerald tried to be encouraging, Tim sounded like all the rest. Roland appeared to be pleading with him; he put his hand on Tim's arm, and Tim shook it off and put his hands in his pockets, looking away across the street. Then Roland must have said something that pacified him, because he shrugged and they came in together.

"It doesn't look too promising," Stephen said.

Roland and Tim stopped for a moment to adjust to the darkness of the cafe.

"Hey, cuz," Roland said brightly. He leaned down and kissed Gerald on the forehead. "And Stephen! You're looking sexy," he said, kissing him.

"It's all the intravenous," Stephen said, smiling in spite of himself.

"I thought so." Roland didn't miss a beat. "Where's John?"

"At his office, I suppose," Gerald said.

"Didn't you invite him?"

"Actually, no." Gerald almost said, *I didn't know it was a party.* "He probably wouldn't have been able to come."

"Well, I wanted you guys to meet Tim," Roland said. "Tim Ketchum."

Tim smiled stiffly and shook their hands.

Roland pulled out a chair for him and Tim sat down reluctantly. "So, did you guys order anything?" Roland asked, still standing. "Cappuccinos? Stephen—you want a cappuccino? Sometimes they don't have a waitress for an hour in the afternoon."

"Sure," Stephen said. Gerald nodded and Roland went up to the counter where a red-haired man came out from the kitchen to wait on him. There was something very proprietary in Roland's casualness that annoyed Gerald.

The three of them sat like stones at the table. Stephen, who would normally have generated a conversation, was tired from his visit to the hospital; Gerald had nothing to say; and Tim Ketchum had already moved his chair out a little way from the table and glanced at his watch.

Roland came back with the coffees and they all sipped quietly. Gerald wanted, suddenly, to see how Roland would navigate through this one. What was he going to say to Stephen, for instance—"How was your treatment?" And if he did actually ask, Stephen might respond with one of his detailed diatribes, and that would surely send Tim Ketchum running for the only exit.

Through the order-up window Gerald saw the back door to the kitchen slam and caught a glimpse of Herminda's black jacket as she came in, confirmed a moment later when he saw the edge of her beat-up bassoon case behind the door, which didn't seem to him like a good spot to store a bassoon. Then he saw a hand on her shoulder, a man's hand, which seemed very large and very white against her black jacket. For a second she came into view, kissing the red-haired man who had made their espressos. Herminda was so lost and relaxed in the embrace, the man's mouth covering hers, that Gerald would not have recognized her. He felt stunned. He thought of the past couple of lessons, which had been sloppy. She'd been distracted and, it seemed, eager to go for the first time.

"That's Mickey," Roland said, having followed Gerald's gaze. "They've been going out for a couple of months now."

Gerald would have glared at Roland, but Mickey was saying something to Herminda and she looked suddenly in their direction. Gerald glanced away quickly as if he hadn't seen her. All four of them were looking her way by that time, so pretending they weren't talking about her made him feel ridiculous.

"That your girl, Gerald?" Stephen asked. There was a chuckle in his voice. Gerald *did* glare at Stephen, and then Herminda was coming toward their table, tying on a small apron that was more like a work belt than an apron. Gerald avoided looking at her until he realized she was avoiding looking at him.

"Herminda," Roland said, familiarly, leaning back in his chair. "I brought the maestro and friends down for a cappuccino."

The maestro. Stephen laughed.

"This is Tim, and Stephen. And the maestro, of course." Tim's smile was as blank and brief as the light signaling the end of intermission, and for a moment Gerald despised everyone at the table and Herminda, too.

She glanced at Gerald for a cue and smiled uneasily. "Can I get you guys something?"

"Actually, yes. I'd like a big plate of nachos," Roland said. "I didn't have lunch. Anyone else?" No one responded, so Herminda wrote down the order and went away.

Tim Ketchum, who had never come in closer than a foot from the table, drained his cappuccino and said he had to be going. "Well, aren't you the busy man?" Roland said brightly, his face falling. Stephen and Gerald grunted their goodbyes and glanced at each other with relief as Roland walked Tim to the door. He was outside on the sidewalk again for a few minutes, and when he came back in he was flushed, probably from arguing again.

"Oh, don't give me the look, either of you," Roland snapped. "We're fighting, okay? I know things about both of *you* you'd rather I didn't reveal."

This was the first time Roland had ever said plainly what had often been on Gerald's mind, but looking now at Stephen's face he realized there was perhaps more that he didn't know.

The nachos arrived. Herminda, wearing a big oven mit, put them and a couple of small plates in front of Roland without looking at anyone and left abruptly. Roland dug into them with his fork. "She's probably ticked that the maestro saw her kissing."

"The *maestro's* probably ticked that he saw her kissing," Stephen blurted.

"Well, people are doing the kiss thing all over the world," Roland said, smiling at this little banter with Stephen.

"Actually," Stephen shrugged, "probably more people *aren't* doing the kiss thing. Most people are alone."

"In that case, Gerald's one of the lucky ones, eh? He's got a man. He should be grateful every time he sees someone kissing because it reminds him of his honey."

They both looked at him, conspiring, but Gerald did not respond.

"Or perhaps he thinks of kissing someone else," Stephen ventured.

"Perhaps he dreams about being in the sack with the two of *us*," Roland said, and they both broke into a laugh. Stephen, relaxing, unzipped his jacket and took a bite of the nachos.

"Nah, not Gerald," Roland continued. "You know what a decent guy he is. That's not the way he lives."

"Actually," Gerald said suddenly, breaking up their prattle, "John's asked for a little...reprieve."

"*What?*" Stephen put his coffee down.

Gerald hadn't meant to blurt it out. He hadn't meant to say anything to anybody until he had a little more time to think about their conversation last night, but somehow Gerald had managed to get through the whole night without thinking about it, just letting his mind skip over it. Even this morning, in the waiting room at the hospital, nothing. Just a blankness. He found himself reading *The New Yorker*, completely absorbed.

"Did he say it that way?" Roland asked. "A *reprieve?*"

Gerald shrugged and leaned away from the table, examining the table's scarred wooden edge. "He just brought up the idea of a little break. What did he say? 'A little time to see what it's like without each other.'"

"He's got someone else in mind," Roland said abruptly. "That's what you say when you want to hook up with someone else but feel too guilty to just do it. It's probably just some kind of mid-life crisis."

"Weren't you ticked?" Roland continued indignantly. "Didn't you, like, tell him to fuck off or something?"

"*No.*"

All through their patient talk on the couch last night, which had ended with "I'll call you in a couple of days" from John, it hadn't occurred to Gerald that John might want to see, or currently be seeing, someone else.

Roland knew how to irritate him more than anyone he knew, Gerald thought. The worst thing was, even now that he'd blurted it out, he felt he should feel more than he did. Perhaps it was a delayed reaction, and perhaps John's new hesitancy *was* a mid-life crisis as Roland said, but whose crisis? Gerald wondered for the first time whether it wasn't he, himself, who was going through the crisis. Not an eruptive crisis, not something that would disturb the evenness of his days, but some other thing, some other commotion that was smothered down in layers of seeming to feel nothing.

"Well, Christ, Gerald, why *wouldn't* he leave if you didn't even want to fight about it?"

"Oh, Roland, shut up and eat your nachos," Stephen said. He leaned over and took Gerald's hand in both of his, without looking at him, and Gerald's eyes filled suddenly with tears. He might lose John, but he would surely lose Stephen.

Herminda came up but took a step back when she saw the expression on Gerald's face. She glanced quickly around the table. "Would you like anything else?" she asked softly.

"No, thanks," Stephen said.

"Will I see you next Wednesday," Gerald managed to say, and Herminda nodded and went to tally the bill.

They dropped Roland off at Market Street, and Gerald drove Stephen home, double-parking in front of the apartment building on 17th. They were quiet a few moments, just listening to the car running, and then Gerald said, trying to sound light, "So what did Roland mean he knew things about *you* he could reveal?"

Stephen shrugged. "We had a thing, a *little* thing, just a few times. After you hooked up with John."

Gerald didn't say anything, thinking about this.

"You're not going to be jealous, are you? I mean, I would've loved a little jealousy from you back then, but you were completely...absorbed. And frankly, the whole thing was—*is*—a little embarrassing."

"Kind of like...sleeping with your son?"

"*No.* Just the kind of embarrassment that comes from being desperate." He paused a second, musing. "Yes, I guess I can say I was desperate."

"I had no idea," Gerald turned to face him.

Stephen shrugged again. "You wouldn't. You were with John. You've got...a *thing*, Gerald. You've got your music. You slept with Roland, but you weren't desperate. I don't have that. And Roland didn't have anything either, really, except a tight little body." One can still appreciate that." He smiled. "Anyhow, I'm not desperate anymore. I'm...something else."

A streetcar coming through clanged at them and Gerald pulled over closer to the parked cars along the curb.

"Don't worry too much about John. He'll figure it out. I bet he'll want to be back with you. I bet. Maybe you need to figure out if you want to be with *him*. Maybe that's your problem."

"I hate you, Stephen." He was about to cry again.

"That's good, because I *love* you." Stephen leaned over and gave Gerald a loud kiss on his ear. "And we wouldn't want things to be out of balance, now, would we? Go ahead and take it hard, Gerald. You can handle it. Drink some Valerian tea and call me tomorrow."

At home Gerald puttered all afternoon. There was some relief in rearranging the sofa cushions and doing laundry. He made sauce for lasagna, which he intended to make tomorrow, and around 7 o'clock he took out his bassoon and worked for a while. He'd agreed to play in a quartet for two concerts next month; the first rehearsal was Monday, and he hadn't even looked at the music. He didn't now. He played just scales, nothing that would demand his full attention, although he could give his full attention to scales.

He tried to think back to when things had begun to be uneasy with John. Since before Thanksgiving, he guessed. They'd been apart for several days while John saw old friends in town, and then went down to San Diego to see his son right after Thanksgiving. Usually he went down only at Christmas and one other time each year. This time when he got back he told Gerald simply, "We need to go out more."

They went to a few parties together over the holidays, but each time Gerald was ready to go before John and almost debated whether to call a cab and go home on his own. John loved to go out; Gerald didn't. This hadn't been a problem before, but now John wanted him to go with him. "You're turning into a curmudgeon," he said. "If you had a picture window, I bet you'd park yourself in front of it and watch the neighbors' comings and goings, and that would be enough for you."

"I have no interest whatsoever in watching the neighbors."

"Exactly."

"Exactly what?"

"No interest. Where's your *interest*, Ger?" He sighed heavily and said, "Listen, I think we should live together, mix up our mess. I can prevent you from becoming an old man. Don't forget—you're a year older than me." John said this in a semi-teasing voice, and they had had sex for the first time in several weeks, but after he left Gerald kept thinking about it.

Then John invited Gerald to San Diego with him for Christmas, but Gerald declined, thinking of John's son, 24, a young officer in the Navy, scrutinizing him—although it hadn't been that way the couple of times Gerald had met him before. Gerald was used to John being gone at Christmas; usually he spent the day with Stephen. They would cook a couple of dishes they hadn't ever done before and listen to music all day, and take a walk. This year, Gerald had felt more restless, drank too much and ended up with a hangover.

When John came back from San Diego, he was very serious. They had a drink, and then he said it, very abruptly, "Ger, if we're not going to live together—if you're not even going to consider it—then maybe we should take a break. Just for a few weeks. See what life is like without each other." He said this quietly, and then met Gerald's eyes. He wasn't backing out of this, or being talked out of it, Gerald saw.

"I've been thinking about it for a while."

"I see."

"No, I don't think you do see. I want to see you without all this...delineation between us. All this coming and going. I want to mix things up. I want, I guess...a little *passion*."

"Well, I can't think of a quicker way of losing passion than moving in together. C'mon, John, we're middle-aged men in our 50's. What kind of passion are you thinking of?" Gerald knew he was right about this. He had thought about it a lot when they first thought of moving in together, several months after they'd met.

John shrugged, and quickly finished the rest of his drink. "Look," he said, getting up, "I'll call you in a couple of days." He avoided Gerald's eyes as he put on his coat.

Roland was probably right; John was probably seeing someone else. Maybe it was his turn for a young fling. Someone like Roland? he wondered. Probably not, probably not that young.

Gerald realized he had been staring out the window with the bassoon across his lap for fifteen minutes. He picked it up and began to play the solo from the beginning of *The Rite of Spring* from memory and stopped. The solo was beautiful, tender, extremely...solitary. What was passion? Not beauty. *Wanting* something. Taken up with want. He thought of Herminda, suddenly, lost in her kiss this afternoon.

Gerald put the horn down and began to take it apart. He wasn't going to play this evening. There was a knock at the door, quick and hesitant. He looked through the peephole and saw

Roland outside. He would have liked to pretend he wasn't home, suddenly dreading whatever crisis Roland might be bringing with him.

"Hi," Roland said as Gerald opened the door. "Can I come in?"

Gerald opened the door wider. Roland smiled briefly and left his jacket on. He glanced around the room, as if for evidence of John.

"He's not here," Gerald said.

"No." Roland shivered. "It's cold outside. I was in the neighborhood. Thought I'd come by."

Gerald thought of mentioning that there were such objects as phones, but he realized he was glad not to be alone just now.

"Were you about to practice?" Roland asked, seeing the bassoon.

"No, just done. I...was going to have a drink," he said. He did not ask whether Roland wanted one, because he knew he did.

"Yes."

He handed Roland a scotch. Roland sipped his drink and watched Gerald as he swabbed the horn out of habit and put each piece in its velvet compartment.

"How come you're not staying over at Timmy's tonight?" The "Timmy" came just out; he hadn't meant to be sarcastic.

Roland frowned. "Tim had to go see his family in El Cerrito. *Some* people have families, as you know," he added. Gerald knew he was trying to dig at him about John's son.

"Not us, though," Roland said. "None of that messy stuff to worry about."

Gerald closed the case, sat down on the couch and crossed his legs.

"Can I stay here tonight?"

Gerald shrugged. "What's the matter with Tim's?"

This time Roland shrugged.

"Yes," Gerald said. "Just tonight, though."

They both sipped their drinks.

"I think I'm going to look into that place Herminda told me about, down the block from her."

"Wasn't that a few months ago? An apartment?"

"A house. It's still vacant; the sign's still up. She said two guys live in it—that means, coming from her, that they're gay—and one of them looks sick. He's always being helped around by the other. She thinks they're looking for someone who can help out."

"Sounds delightful."

"*Jesus*, Gerald."

"Okay, sorry. I'm in a mood."

"You were *born* in a mood, I think. Sometimes."

Gerald ignored him and got up to fix another drink. "Why don't you put on a Duraflame?" he said to Roland. "They're in the closet outside the front door."

Gerald took out some turkey breast he had frozen and put it in the microwave while Roland lit the paper-covered log.

"It says here two-and-a-half hours. Two and a half hours of romantic log-light."

Gerald snorted. "Have you eaten?"

"Why do you always ask that when you know I never have?"

Gerald flapped his hand at him. "I've got some turkey coming up."

Roland took off his jacket and sat on the floor. They ate hot turkey sandwiches in silence in front of the fire. The room was oddly peaceful; it reminded Gerald vaguely of when Roland had first come to the city, that first week when he was staying here.

Only then it was spring, and they had looked out the window instead of at a fire.

"What are you thinking of?"

"Why do you ask."

"You had a look on your face."

Gerald shrugged. "Actually, I was thinking about when you first came here."

"Me, too." He paused. "That wasn't so bad, was it, Gerald?"

Gerald shrugged again. "No, not then."

"John and Tim have families. We don't have any of that messy stuff to worry about, Gerald; we've got each other." Roland got up off the floor and plopped down in the chair across from him, holding up his glass.

"To each other," Gerald said, lifting his glass briefly, smirking. He felt suddenly very drunk.

"Each *other*," Roland replied. "Brother. Mother."

"Smother," Gerald said.

"Yes, smother. Smother me please. Smother me another nutter butter peanut butter sandwich cookie..." Roland did an old television commercial spin-off and Gerald began to laugh, a laugh that came up through him and wouldn't stop even though the joke wasn't that funny—there wasn't even a joke, really— and the funny look on Roland's face made him laugh even harder, tears coming out of his eyes, and then he spilled his scotch. He sat up, still laughing, and Roland went for a sponge and sopped it off the floor. Gerald watched him clean up.

"Geez, you guys really must have had some fight," Roland said, pouring Gerald another drink—this would be number three—and Gerald thought for a second how much Roland knew instinctively—how he'd *always* known things, even back then at 16—while he himself had to sit and analyze a situation and come to a conclusion. He envied Roland his instincts. It wasn't intuition; it was instinct. Because Roland had always had to get by.

"Not a fight," he said.

"Oh, right. You guys don't fight. A discussion of some sort. Don't want to get too much wet passion going on."

"Don't you think that perhaps a *discussion* as you so sarcastically put it is better than yelling, or slamming each other around?" The edge the scotch had made was crumbling and Gerald felt irritated like he had before.

Roland shrugged.

Gerald put his drink on the coffee table harder than he meant to. "I'm irritated," he said, rubbing his eyes.

Roland got up and went behind the couch and began to rub Gerald's shoulders. He pushed his hand away, but Roland persisted. The massage felt good and he just sat there quietly for a few minutes until Roland stopped and went back to his chair.

"I like it when you laugh like that," Roland said. "I've never seen you laugh like that." He bit a fingernail, scrutinizing Gerald. "I wouldn't worry about you and John," he said. "He'll be back."

"I'm not sure I want him to come back."

"What? Are you crazy?"

"I think, maybe, that I wanted things to change. Not for him to leave, maybe, but for things to change."

"What things?"

"I don't know." Gerald shrugged. "Thanks for the rub. I'm going to bed. You know where the sheets are."

Roland nodded. There was a look in his eyes, but Gerald ignored it and went to bed. After a few minutes he heard the television click on and drifted off to the muffled noise.

He awoke suddenly from a deep sleep about an hour later, thinking someone had called his name. Squinting across the dark room, he saw Roland, shirtless, in the doorway. Roland didn't speak or move toward him and Gerald knew if he didn't say anything to him, Roland would come to bed. Quite suddenly his whole body ached for him, in a way it hadn't in six years. Stephen was wrong. He *had* been desperate, and now it was more of a memory than a feeling.

He pulled the sheet up over his shoulders. "No, Roland," he said, simply, and Roland stood there another few seconds and left, closing the door behind him. Gerald heard the TV click on again, and eventually he fell back asleep. The next morning Roland was gone, and Gerald had a feeling he wouldn't see him again for a while.

Chapter 10

Herminda loved the high, sweet sound of the Lead Muleteer's voice as he sang *"Little bird, little bird, do you sing for me?"* into the empty theater. She didn't much care for the man playing Don Quixote, however; a local actor who'd made a couple of commercials in Los Angeles and took himself very seriously. He had already spent part of the dress rehearsal arguing, again, with the director about pacing in the windmill scene. The flute followed the melody, and Herminda felt a camaraderie when she came in, without a squeak, echoing the flute's notes on her bassoon, two octaves lower.

Gerald was right; she had to do something, something in a group, and so she had taken BART over to Berkeley and auditioned for the University's production of *Man of La Mancha*. No other bassoonists auditioned, and she had gotten the part.

"Goddammed stupid, a musical in the middle of February, if you ask me," Gertz, the conductor, had grumbled to no one in particular the first rehearsal in the middle of January. They had all dragged chairs into the empty orchestra pit and introduced themselves. Ralph Gertz was short and stout and mostly bald, and except for his girth he reminded Herminda of Gerald. He played clarinet in the San Francisco Symphony, and Herminda guessed Gertz must be in need of money, since he obviously wasn't too happy about being involved in a rinky-dink college production.

But everyone in the small orchestra was friendly and competent, and after they'd gone through the score a couple of times at the first rehearsal, Gertz was more relaxed. Herminda had been anxious about playing with a group for the first time since high school, but no one paid much attention to her and she was able to observe without feeling observed herself. Except for one of the flutists, who was Asian, she was the only non-white person in the orchestra, and the only one who wasn't playing with some other group. Most of the small orchestra were students at the University, except for the percussionist, who played with a local rock band and the San Francisco Symphony. Herminda remembered him from the concert Gerald had given her tickets to. He looked interesting. Maybe gay, she thought. He could be anything, with his long dark hair pulled back in a ponytail, earrings, and tight, all-black outfits. She overheard the clarinetist say that the percussionist was getting paid for playing. "I think Gertz is in love with him," he snickered.

"Bassoon, you're sharp," Gertz said as they finished the last song. He constantly forgot their names and had taken to addressing them as their instruments. It had been a long evening and everyone was tired. She pulled the reed off the Fox, blew it dry, and wiped it with a cloth that she slid back underneath her thigh. She did not look forward to the ride on BART back to the city. After the first rehearsal, Mickey had begun driving her to Berkeley, claiming he didn't like the idea of her out with her bassoon on BART late at night. She didn't protest. He said it might the only time he ever got to see her play, and when she told him he couldn't just sit around during rehearsals, he said he had errands he could do. Last time he'd brought Christopher with them and they'd gone out for ice cream while she rehearsed. Tonight he had to work, but he'd gotten a babysitter for the performance Saturday night.

"Dressy and dark," Gertz reminded them of their performance attire when the dress rehearsal was over. He passed out two complimentary tickets to each person who wanted them. "*Dresses* for the women, please," he said, and Herminda thought that Gertz gazed at her a moment longer than the others. She would show him, if he was. Last weekend she and Mickey had gone downtown, to Macy's, and he'd bought her a black dress. "If I buy it," he'd said, "it has to be something I at least *like*." She wasn't sure if this meant he distrusted her taste, and it ticked her off a little, but then they found a perfect, plain dress— lightweight black wool, long-sleeved and scooped out to the middle of her back, knee-length with a full skirt. She knew she would never have even noticed the dress if Mickey weren't with her. It wasn't her style—if she *had* a style, she thought. It was what her sister would call a "lady" dress. Before he took her shopping Herminda had planned on borrowing one of Silvia's black dresses and cinching it with a black belt. But Mickey had asked her what she was supposed to wear and protested. "Herminda, you'll be doing this more than once. You need a dress."

"What about...you know," she put her hand on her chest wondering about a bra as she scrutinized the dress in the mirror at the store.

"Nothing," Mickey said. "Just you." He glanced both ways before coming behind her and running his big hands over her breasts and down her dress as they both watched in the mirror. "You don't need anything," he said, which was true. Her breasts were small and round beneath the soft wool.

At the counter a saleswoman said they had low-backed bras, if she was interested. "Maybe later," Herminda had said, biting her lip to keep from giggling.

"And forty-five minutes early," Gertz was saying. "Be here. Let's do well."

Herminda took her time packing up her horn since Mickey wasn't coming, and soon it was just a couple of stagehands organizing scenery on the stage, herself and the drummer in the pit. She watched him pack his snare into the hatbox-shaped case and looked around the almost empty auditorium.

"Think there'll be anyone here tomorrow night besides parents and grandparents?" Herminda mused aloud.

The drummer shrugged and tossed his ponytail over his shoulder as he snapped the case shut. "Who else would go to a production like *Man of La Mancha*?" she said.

"You never know," he said.

"So you do speak," she said boldly.

He shrugged again, but smiled, which made him a much more attractive person. He was younger than she'd thought. There were a few rough spots on the edge of his jaw where he had shaved some whiskers off, but mostly his skin was still smooth and hairless. Herminda noticed a faint line of freckles on the skin beneath his nose.

"You play with the Symphony?"

"Yeah."

"So this must be easy for you."

"It's easy for you, too. Should be easy for everyone." Shrugging was apparently as eloquent as he could get.

"What is your name?" she asked.

"Alec Coughlin."

"I'm Herminda Matta," she said, extending her hand. She saw the door at the top of the auditorium open from the corner of her eye.

He shook her hand lightly and smiled, embarrassed.

"There's a rumor you're getting paid to do this," Herminda said.

Alec chuckled. His whole demeanor changed when he smiled, almost like another person, and she could see he was much more self-confident than he initially portrayed himself. "Well, I'm not. I'm doing it as a favor to Gertz."

So maybe he *was* connected to Gertz. "I haven't played with a group since high school," Herminda offered.

"Oh," he said.

She'd hoped he would say more—that she was good, or that he'd heard she was going to play with the Symphony in the spring, although this wasn't yet confirmed. He probably hadn't even noticed her. She felt jealous of him, so young, playing professionally.

"Hey," Alec said, taking his complimentary tickets from his leather jacket, "you need any more tickets? I don't know why I took these."

Herminda took them, even though she could not think of anyone besides Mickey who would come. She tried to picture her mother at *Man of La Mancha*. Her mother would not understand it and might even be offended. "Well, you said you never know who'll show up," she said.

"You see? Obviously, *someone's* coming. Well, I think I'd better get going," Alec said, tilting his head toward the security guard looking down on them from the top row of auditorium seats. "I have to make two trips to the car."

"Are you going to the city?"

"Yeah."

Herminda hesitated.

"Need a ride?" he asked.

She nodded. "If you don't mind."

"No problem."

"Can I help you with those cases?"

"Looks like you've got a big enough one of your own."

Herminda took one of his cases and stood in the lobby while Alec ran down to the pit twice to collect the rest of his drums. "That's probably what I should get," he said, nodding to Herminda's luggage tote. Then she waited with the equipment while Alec got his car and pulled up to the front of the auditorium.

"Well, it's a help having you hang out with the stuff. Usually I ask the security guy to wait around, but by the time I get the car pulled up he's off somewhere. I don't appreciate that," he said, loading up the forest green Volvo stationwagen so quickly that suddenly he was done and had his hands out for her horn. He took it lightly, as if it were empty, and slid it along the tops of his cases.

"And now," he said, "we have to get some coffee. For the road. I need to be awake by the time I hit the city." Alec drove fast enough down Telegraph Avenue to come to a screech as he double-parked in front of a cafe. He would've made a good cab driver, she thought. Or a bad one.

On New Year's Day, Mickey had attempted to teach her how to drive in the huge, deserted parking lot at the Serramonte shopping mall. They had jerked their way around the lot, starting and stopping abruptly until Christopher had begun to whine from the backseat and Mickey said (a bit irritated, she'd thought), "Let's call it a day."

"New Year's Day!" Christopher had piped.

Alec turned to her. "What do you want?" he said. The question was asked so abruptly that Herminda didn't understand what he meant.

"Cappuccino? Latte?"

"Oh, I'm fine." She thought she might like a latte, decaffeinated, but she didn't want to ask.

"I'll just be a second, but here's the keys just in case." He was assuming she knew how to drive. Herminda sat tensely in the car for the two minutes it took Alec to come back with two drinks.

"That was awfully fast," she said, holding the drinks for him as he pulled out into traffic.

He shrugged. "They know me. I got you a latte. Decaf."

"I wanted one."

"Well, I must have heard your inner self saying 'Gimme a latte decaf.'" He chuckled softly, and the strange phrase *Gimme a latte decaf* made her wonder, suddenly, what Alec would say when he was making love. For the past two months she found herself thinking about sex almost constantly, except when she was playing music, and even then the knowledge of it, of her body, of what she was part of, made playing music easier. She didn't usually think of Mickey when she thought of sex; it was a more generalized thinking. What it was like for other people, she wondered, and scrutinized them differently now when she was in the café or the produce shop. How strange that so many people did this thing! She had always been curious, but she had never thought it would ever be something she would *want*. It was then that she would think of Mickey. Several people had commented on how she looked different, that she was looking good. Her uncle had kidded her about having a man in her life, not knowing anything about Mickey, and she blushed. Silvia had offered to show her how to do her lips so they looked bigger and asked her if she was going to go on the pill, and without waiting for a response told her about the clinic on Army Street where she could get a prescription. Mickey was taking care of that for now. He said he didn't like the idea of her having to take hormones.

Herminda looked at Alec's thin, long-fingered hands on the steering wheel. Had he had a lot of lovers? She was embarrassed thinking about it. He put his hand out toward her for the coffee. His fingers were warm.

"So," he said, pulling off the exit toward the Bay Bridge, "Gertz tells me you'll be playing with the Symphony in the spring concert."

She was pleased that they both knew. "Yeah, just one concert."

"Don't you love that piece of music, *Rite of Spring*?" Alec said. He made some explosive sounds with his mouth that Herminda vaguely recognized as the percussion near the beginning, and she laughed. Then he sang the opening bassoon solo with a twang like an oboe.

"That's very good," she said, still chuckling.

They were quiet a few moments. She loved coming toward the city from the Bay Bridge and missed the ride when she had to go underground. The Embarcadero buildings, outlined in lights all year now, rose up dramatically in front of them.

"I always think they look like piano keys," Alec said about the buildings, as if following her thoughts.

"Broken piano keys."

"Yeah." He was quiet a moment. "So, you said you aren't playing with a group. Are you going to try out anywhere?"

Herminda shrugged. "I don't know. I don't have any credentials. No college." These were things she'd chosen not to think about. She didn't feel ready.

"What do *you* do when you're not playing?" she asked.

"I play in a local band called the Endzones. Rock. Some spacey things...."

Herminda shook her head; she hadn't heard of the group.

"But that's playing, isn't it, and you asked about not-playing," he said, and laughed.

"It is," she said. Perhaps the coffee had kicked in; he drummed the steering wheel with his thin fingers.

"Well, actually, I don't have a job right now. I got a grant, just a little one, to compose some music—which I haven't quite done yet—and I've been living off it. I'm hoping to hold off until the symphony checks start coming in. I'm not really on the payroll until fall."

It was hard to believe someone so young could get a grant to write music and get into the orchestra. He wasn't older than 26. Herminda wondered how much he would make playing in the Symphony.

"Hey, you know," he said, "I'm composing a few pieces for my band, and we could use a bassoon. I could write you in."

"A bassoon in a rock band?"

"Sure, why not? Moondog did it."

"Moondog?"

"Never mind. It's a great sound, I think. We could do some jazzy pieces if you're up to it."

"Well—"

"Think about it."

"Well, sure." Herminda tried to imagine herself in Alec's apartment or garage somewhere, with a saxophone player and someone on keyboards. They'd have to put a mic on her horn or it would be like she wasn't playing at all. She liked the idea; her body warmed with nervousness imagining the possibility.

Alec was quiet the rest of the way. She told him she lived on Florida Street and Alec maneuvered them through the Mission with ease without further directions. He double-parked again and unloaded her bassoon for her. "Thank you," she said.

"Well, see you tomorrow night. And at rehearsal in a couple months," he said. He smiled lopsidedly and pointed his finger at her. "Be there." Obviously he liked her well enough. Did he find her at all attractive? She wanted to know.

The TV was on in the front room and Ricardo was sprawled out on the couch with a beer in his hand and a couple of cans on the table in front of him. He hadn't been around much in the past few weeks, but his shoes were off and it appeared that he would be staying the night.

"So's that the little faggot boyfriend?" he said, snidely. "Must weigh about as much as you."

"*No*, that's not my boyfriend." Ricardo must have been watching them through the blinds. Herminda wondered whether she should give her brother the satisfaction of an explanation or just walk away.

"He's a drummer. He plays in the Symphony and gave me a ride home." Ricardo, she realized, would probably have an even lower opinion of Mickey, who was so white and friendly.

"Takes care of the little horn-player. The little horny player," Ricardo snickered.

Herminda started to leave the room.

"Sorry, Minda. I didn't mean it. You can hang out with anyone you want. You're a big girl now, I hear."

She paused at the door, disliking the undertones in her brother's voice. Silvia must have been talking to him. The room was very dark except for the bluish flickering of the television, at which Ricardo continued to stare.

"For your information, I got laid off today," he said. "Can't fucking believe it. I actually liked that job." Ricardo had been working at an auto parts store on Mission Street near Army for almost six months now. Their mother had been so proud and enthusiastic about him being employed that Herminda and Silvia gotten tired of hearing her go on and on about him.

"Did you tell Mama?"

"Nah. Maybe I'll have another one before next week. Felix said I can work on a couple of body jobs with him."

Whenever Herminda heard Felix's name, she glazed over it, not thinking of the person, just the name.

"Don't you tell her," Ricardo said.

"I won't say anything." She paused. Slouched on the sofa, his stomach showing where his flannel shirt was unbuttoned, Herminda had an image of what her brother would be like in ten years. She wondered if he looked like their father. His skin was lighter than any of theirs. If he cleaned up, and changed his hairstyle, and spoke English all the time, you might even think he was white. It would've been easier for him, was all, she thought, biting her lip. Easier if he was white. Easier for all of them, maybe, but especially him.

"I'm sorry about your job, brother," she said quietly, and put her hand on his shoulder. Ricardo grabbed it and squeezed it but did not turn his attention from the television.

"Yeah, well," was all he said.

Herminda dropped her jaw for low A as the orchestra tuned for the first performance. There had been a message from Gerald on her answering machine that afternoon wishing her luck. She was glad he remembered. Things hadn't been quite the same between them since that afternoon he and Roland and those other two men had come to the café and saw her kissing Mickey. Herminda didn't know if she would trace this back to the kiss if Roland hadn't brought it up the week after they had been there.

"So how's it going with Gerald?" Roland had asked, sipping his daily cappuccino on the way home from his job at the brokerage downtown.

"Fine," she said.

"I was just wondering. I think he was really blown away when he saw you making out in the kitchen. His little Herminda, with some other life than playing bassoon." Roland shook his head and clucked sarcastically.

Herminda wondered if this was true. And over the next few weeks she did notice a difference. Both she and Gerald acted the same, but there was a certain distance now. Maybe it had always been there? she wondered, but no, there was something different. He was more critical and at the same time he avoided watching her. He had sat whole lessons with his chair parallel to hers, never turning toward her unless he had to show her something. She was tempted to ask him what was wrong, but what if he said "Nothing"—would *she* bring up the kitchen episode? She didn't like feeling ignored and scrutinized at the same time.

And she didn't like the way Roland was so gleeful about it. When she wasn't at the café, Roland had taken to talking to Mickey and now it was almost like the two of them were friends. And Roland *was* friendly. It was just the way he seemed to know a lot more about her life than she knew about his, or wanted to know. She distrusted the way Roland's desires seemed to spread all over, strong but unspecific. They were from different worlds; what did he want with hers?

He lived closer now, too. A couple of weeks ago, he'd moved into the house at the end of the block that Herminda had told him about. The rent was cheap, Roland said, in exchange for helping with the sick man, whose lover had an antique shop and had to be out of the house for a while every day. He hadn't been their first choice for a housemate because of his work hours, but the other candidate bowed out at the last moment. There wasn't that much to do—checking on the man, whose name was Joe, helping him into bed. So far, even though Roland called out "Howdy, neighbor" when he came into the café, Herminda hadn't seen him any more than before.

Mickey had offered Roland a ticket and a ride to the performance, but Roland canceled at the last minute, with apologies. Herminda was relieved.

"He really likes you, Minda," Mickey said on their drive to Berkeley.

"I know he likes me, and he's a nice enough guy. Sometimes I feel like I'm some way for him to get at Gerald. I don't know why. Or what he'd be getting at."

"You've got to introduce me to Gerald sometime." It was the first time they had dressed up together, and she liked the way he looked with a navy jacket and tie and his hair combed back. "I almost wore the tie with the musical notes on it, but I decided not to," he said. She was glad; she didn't want him to look funny. "Sometime I should probably meet your mother, too," he said, but she didn't answer and he didn't say more. Her mother knew she was seeing someone but had been very quiet about it. She'd praised Herminda's dress and wished her good luck on the way out, but Herminda didn't care to predict what her mother would think of Mickey.

The last performance of *Man of La Mancha* came off without a hitch. Herminda saw Mickey in the audience before the lights went down and gave him a tentative wave. She was aware of playing particularly for him and it made her feel confident. Of course, the music was not difficult, she reminded herself, so it was easy to feel confident. From her position in the pit, she could only see part of the stage. On one side of the orchestra Herminda could feel the thumps of comings and goings through the wooden floor. On the other side, she felt the weight of the audience in the darkness of the small auditorium, its breathing and fidgeting and little responses to the action onstage. There were a couple of mis-cues, but after half an hour the production had hit its stride and was going smoothly. The auditorium exploded into laughter at the windmill scene when Quixote crawled back onstage, but Herminda willed herself not to let her attention drift onto the audience since she'd missed a cue the first night, distracted by all the people. She caught Alec's eye and he smiled at her. Ralph Gertz appeared both pleased and relieved; the happy, mostly high school audience gave a standing ovation, and she overheard some of the other orchestra members planning to go out for drinks at a bar on the north side of Berkeley.

Afterward, Alec approached her as she was cleaning her bassoon. "So," he said, "that's over. Would you like to go out with a few of us for a drink?"

The idea of going out was appealing, although she was worried about her ID, and then she remembered Mickey waiting for her in the lobby.

"Thanks, but I have to go."

"How are you getting home?"

She shrugged. "I have someone waiting for me."

Alec smiled slyly. "Well, see you in a few weeks, then."

"This is my QUEST, to follow that STARrrr," Mickey sang, rolling the *r*, as they drove over the Bay Bridge. "Actually, you know, Quixote *was* kind of an Inquisition-era homeless man."

"Yeah, I suppose so," Herminda answered. She felt restless and was wishing she could have stayed to go out for drinks with the others.

"You okay?" Mickey touched her arm.

"Just tired."

Mickey pulled up and parked down the block from the house and stopped the engine. "That was fun," he said. He looked at her and suddenly the car filled with the energy that spilled all around them when they made love. Tonight, though, it was different. Herminda was conscious of wanting to make love, just wanting, and for the first time it was not attached particularly to wanting Mickey. It was like a separate being in the car.

"Look, why don't you come in. If she's up," she said, referring to her mother, "you can meet her. If she's not, well," Herminda shrugged, "you can see my room."

The flat was dark, and they came in quietly. She knew Ricardo would not be home tonight. They could hear the low murmur from her mother's television and Herminda knew she was asleep. They passed Silvia's door. In a way, she wanted Silvia to see her, to hear her making love, but she doubted that Silvia would be in before midnight. Herminda took Mickey by the hand and led him to her room, latching the door behind her, and when she turned in the dark he had her in his arms. His mouth on her neck made her entire body feel like there was an electrical current going through it. She loved that feeling.

"I want to make love to you with that dress on," he whispered, running his hands over her hips, kneeling in front of her like the first time, pulling down her tights.

She didn't like the idea of her dress getting rumpled, or damp from their bodies. "No," she said, and slipped it off her shoulders. The room was cold, and she took his hand and led him to her narrow bed. She turned on the radio to muffle their whispers. She sat on the edge of the bed and unzipped his pants and let them fall, then took his hand and pulled him onto the bed with her.

Were other people together this easily? she wondered. From television, from her sisters, from her mother, from the girls at school, it didn't sound like it. When she was making love with Mickey, it was like going far away into an inner world. His body was so much larger than hers, but gentle, enveloping, and she loved how he could engulf her but she still held him tight with herself, feeling safe and wild at the same time. Sometimes Herminda did wonder what it would be like with a different man. The thing with Mickey was that she trusted him. Could you trust someone and not love them? Not be in-love with them?

"I love you, Herminda," Mickey whispered, as if trying to answer her question, but she could not say it back. In the background she heard the keys rattling and thump of the front door as Silvia came home. Mickey hesitated, but it was too late, and Herminda let herself cry out, hoping her mother was asleep but wanting Silvia to hear, wanting her sister to know that she had something for herself now, too.

Chapter 11

"If you're not calling him, why should he call you?" Stephen asked. He had invited Gerald for dinner but at the last minute was too tired to make it, so they had gone out and picked up some Vietnamese food to go. Now they sat on the floor in the tiny living room of Stephen's apartment finishing the ginger chicken. It was Sunday night. Both Roland and John had been in their conversation, and so for a moment Gerald wasn't sure which "him" Stephen meant. He guessed John.

"I don't know," Gerald said. He wished they'd eaten at his house. There were trays of medications in both the bedroom and the bathroom; the kitchenette was dingy and the furniture in the living room was uncomfortable, which was why they were sitting side by side on the floor. The place was cramped and cluttered, and the whole apartment was a reminder to Gerald that Stephen had AIDS.

Stephen's computer in the corner was on most of the time. Apparently there was some sort of online AIDS hotline that he subscribed to, with news releases, question-and-answer forums, and, of course, people who wanted to start up online correspondence. Stephen claimed he might even be able to toss out a lot of the medical magazines and some of the newsletters that were scattered around his apartment since he could get the information on his machine. It was all part of the world Stephen was more and more involved in. As he was less and less a part of this world, Gerald thought.

"I am an ass," he said.

"I won't disagree," Stephen replied, licking his fingers.

"Your whole apartment reminds me you're sick."

"Yeah. Me, too," Stephen said promptly. He grabbed Gerald's arm and leaned against him affectionately for a moment.

"I *am* an ass," Gerald said again.

Stephen sighed. "Look, we were talking about John. It's been almost three months. You said you'd met him for dinner four times. Of course, did you ever mention any of these dinners to me during our many phone conversations. *Nooooo.* I have to guess what's going on in your life. You say you didn't want to bore me. Well, it would seem to me that your *love* life would be of some priority. Especially since you have no other life, except for that goddammed horn of yours. What did you *say* at those dinners?"

Gerald sighed. Stephen seemed determined to converse about John, probably as a way to keep from talking about himself. The conversations were more like chit-chat than real discussion. Perhaps because there was nothing to discuss, or perhaps because it was all part of this overall syndrome, this null-and-voidness.

"It was like it was before, really. I liked being with him. We laughed. It wasn't tense. The only thing different was that we left each other outside the restaurant."

"How cozy." Stephen was clicking his chopsticks together in an annoying way. "Who asked who out?"

"I called him once."

"So he called three times."

"I don't think he was tallying."

"Wanna make a bet? Haven't you talked about what you want? Or what he wants, anyway?"

"I presume he is waiting for me to say something. And, frankly, I don't know what to say because I don't know how I feel. I feel...*numb*. I feel like nothing. I feel like I feel nothing." Stephen was about to interrupt him, but he held up his hand. "I feel, probably, mostly, guilty."

"Oh, guilt, guilt. Guilt's no good."

"Guilty that I don't feel more?" Gerald went on, smirking. "Other than that, I can't tell if I'm happy or sad. I'm neither. I mean, at home, I'm lonely. I miss him coming over. I know something's missing. But I'm not in *pain* over it. Maybe some people—maybe even *most* people are just fine without being in love."

"Oh, God, Gerald," Stephen said, getting up slowly. "You're worse than I thought. You're fucking *unhopeful*. Practically...existential." He took Gerald's plate and his own and shuffled to the kitchen and put them in the sink.

"I did call him again, Stephen."

"What? *Now* you tell me."

"I called him the day before yesterday. His office said he was in San Diego on business and would be back Thursday."

"So he didn't even tell you he was going out of town?"

"Why should he?"

"Yeah. Right."

He would get Stephen a weekly maid service, Gerald thought. He could afford that, and Stephen's place needed it.

"You could use some of my mood elevators." Stephen shook a small brown plastic bottle. "Don't worry. No refills. Geez, *I* might have to take one now, after listening to you." He smiled weakly, his face drawn and tired, and Gerald's eyes filled suddenly with tears. Stephen either didn't see his sadness or chose to ignore it, turning to the cupboard. "How about some coffee instead. I *can* make coffee. Here. Open your fortune cookie." He tossed a cellophane package across the room.

"Fortune cookies? I thought it was Vietnamese."

"Go figure. Maybe the owner's Chinese."

"*You know who you are. Follow your star,*" Gerald read.

"See. There it is. A little poem."

"A little poem."

"Poetry. Along with the medication, you could use a little poetry in your life, Poulin."

At 10 o'clock Stephen was tired and they parted at the door, Gerald embracing him longer than usual. "Let go of me, Poulin," Stephen said gruffly. "I'm not going anywhere *this* week. You're picking me up tomorrow, correct? Good night."

Gerald stood on the stoop a couple of minutes. Stephen seemed actually glad to get rid of him. Perhaps *he* was becoming a burden to Stephen. The thought made him more depressed. Behind him one of the bay windows opened.

"Psst, Gerald! The neighbors will be talking if you don't get out of here. You're the third man today to stand on my porch looking dazed. Go home!" Stephen laughed and shut the window, blowing him a kiss, and Gerald felt better.

It was a damp night, and chilly. He waited at the corner of 17th for a streetcar. When he had walked down from Hill Street four hours earlier, there was still light in the sky, a surprisingly clear night for the end of March. He'd paused at the top of Dolores Park, which was the same view as the one from his deck, but closer. Half in shadow, the Bay Bridge sparkled, and the hills of the East Bay were tinged pink. But now all that was shut down, he thought. What a way to think of a day, *shutting down*, as though the night weren't full of activity. But maybe only activity here, in the city. John had brought up the idea once of moving north somewhere, to the country, but had finally decided against it. To find "country" in California now you had to go too far. Too far to commute, anyway. And John liked his evening forays, Gerald thought. Certainly more than he himself did, who had never really considered moving from the city and probably never would.

Mist made a hissing noise on the electric wires, and Church Street was surprisingly quiet. Gerald thought about the first rehearsal for the spring concert on Wednesday. Everything was in place. Cynthia would be out until the fall. She had had a son last Friday. Gerald received the little announcement yesterday; he'd have to get a gift of some sort. He should have asked Stephen what would be appropriate. Herminda seemed comfortable enough with the music, although they hadn't gone through the Rossini more than a couple of times. And Richard hadn't been too thrilled to learn he'd be on third bassoon for *Rite*. "She needs the experience," Gerald had explained to him, "and she's quite good." Time to put Richard in his place a bit, maybe force him to move on. Leonard remained his gruff, quiet self on contra-bassoon. What an odd quartet they would make, Gerald mused.

He looked at his watch, estimating that he'd been waiting ten minutes for the streetcar, and sighed. He sighed all the time these days. A young man with blond hair in a white, full-body spandex suit jogged by, acknowledging Gerald with a little nod. He watched him fade into the drifting fog like some kind of fluorescent angel. The man made him think of Roland. As he expected, Roland had not called him since that night in early January, nor had he called Roland, and he didn't think about it except occasionally. Roland wanted something from everyone, and Gerald had no desire to give. Herminda said he'd moved in down the block from her, but she didn't see him either, except at the café.

The fog bank was tunneling down 17th Street toward him like a wave in slow motion, and Gerald felt a sudden urge to avoid it, to get above it, and decided to walk home instead of waiting for the train. A little uphill would be good for him. That's what Stephen would say. A little uphill. Along with a little poetry. Yes, he remembered, and medication.

If he was in San Diego, Gerald mused, John would probably stay with his son. But maybe not. Maybe he'd stay in a hotel and just have dinner a couple of times with him. Gerald had often tried to imagine John as a young father. He was so conscientious and full of goodwill that it wasn't hard. Harder to imagine him in bed with a woman. On that subject, John hadn't had much to say. "Just so...soft," he'd said. "Too soft for me. I always thought I'd lose myself, just dissolve, in her. But not losing myself like passion. More like fear." But he'd stayed with his wife until Michael was 14, and was newly divorced when he met Gerald.

What was it that John had wanted in him? With him? From him? He couldn't get his prepositions correct.

Gerald tried to think again of the Wednesday rehearsal. He'd pick up Herminda. The last time he'd played *The Rite of Spring* was before he'd met John. He was lonely most of the time back then, but the music took the edge off that. He had performed with a few small ensembles on the side, and spent a lot of time with Stephen, who had a recordings collection to rival Gerald's. They used to sit up late, drinking and arguing over conducting styles and the tempo of this passage or that. They were very full of themselves. Gerald had never understood why Stephen didn't take up an instrument. Stephen claimed lack of talent, and lack of interest. He wanted the big picture, the completed whole, he said. He didn't want to work at it; that's what he said.

Every time he tried to think of John, he ended up thinking about Stephen. Every time he tried to think of the music, he ended up thinking of Stephen. Stephen was the only thing that brought up any emotions in him, he thought. Stephen, who might not live out the year. What would he do without him? What would he do?

Gerald had paused in the middle of the sidewalk, breathing heavier from the uphill grade. He turned automatically to look at the view again. The tiny lights shimmered, and he realized he was crying. He wiped his face with the back of his hand. Pity and rot, he thought. An ass. Think of the music. The music might have helped. If he could go over it enough, like Herminda did, going over it all in her head. A different kind of practice. He hadn't made any comment, but he was impressed that she did that, that she made that work for her. Imaginary practice. Of course, everything was still so new for her, everything. The rehearsal Wednesday would be a big day.

A foghorn blared, then faded, drowned out by the rumble of the streetcar he could have been on as it headed toward the bend at the top of the park.

The first section of *Rite*. The opening bassoon solo that started off so sweet, and sad— "A Kiss of the Earth," it was called. A little prayer, Gerald thought, surprising himself. He pictured the score in his mind and went over each note under his breath, approaching the steepest part of the hill.

The streetlight was out. He sensed it behind him, first a slicing in the air, and then the chain wrapped around his face and he went down on his knees. "Hey! *Cocksucker!*" one of them yelled jubilantly.

He tried to get to his feet when the chain whipped across his back. There were two of them, he saw, blurrily, kids, one tall, one short, both skinny, both tight and wired. He couldn't tell whether they each had a stick and chain, or just one of them. Now they were quiet, pacing around him like animals around prey. Gerald wanted to yell; like a dream where the scream won't come out. He tried to get up again, half on the sidewalk now and half on the street, but the arm rose and the chain wrapped around his face again and he fell face down.

Kiss of the earth, he thought, pebbles from the street sticking to his bloody lips.

To lie there with his arms covering his head. He wanted to sleep, submit. Maybe they would go away. But the chain came across his back and now a noise did come from him; a yell of some sort; practically a bark. He came to his feet faster than they expected and half-staggered across the street, toward the lit side, hollering, his ears ringing. He wanted the sound of a window opening, or a door. They came up on either side of him and one chain came around his forehead and slipped down. He couldn't see; and then it came snapping around again. He tasted metal and blood in his mouth; the side of his face was wet; and still he kept thinking *Scream*, and he did, a sound like a low moan echoing through his skull, as if he were underwater. He pulled against the stick with the chain wrapped around his face, trying to stay on his feet. Almost floating. They were viciously quiet, as though they were concentrating, as though they were at *work*, he thought vaguely; they might kill him. They might kill him. One of them kicked him in the butt as he stumbled toward the center of the street. They were talking to each other. Arguing. A car, perhaps—*anything*. Where was everyone? The chain slipped off his face again and he yelled. Even as a door finally opened—oh, the flicker of the light the yellow glow of a hallway streaming onto the street, warm, so... warm—"Please!" he called out. And even as a man came out onto the sidewalk, cautious, and said loudly, "What's going on out here?", the kids did not run but stood near Gerald, half in the street, as though debating whether or not to hit him again, not seeing the man in the doorway as a threat. Finally, one of them said tensely, "C'*mon*, Ricardo," and something else hissed, and Gerald turned to look at them. It was a blur; one eye was dimmed and not seeing; but he saw the tall one, saw the stick with the chain on the end of it, and the kid stepped up close to him, the black eyes completely without regard, somehow familiar, very close, and Gerald trembled, unable to move. "Fucking faggot. You know what you are." Each word a pierce. Gerald bent over from the middle and vomited in the street, trying to move across toward that light, and then they were gone.

The man and his wife did not bring him into their house. They called the police, and the man waited with him outside on the sidewalk, pacing cautiously until they came. Perhaps he and his wife thought he had something to do with the fight, that he was somehow involved. Or perhaps they felt the same way as the muggers about homosexuals. Or perhaps they didn't want blood spots in their foyer. The woman brought out a dishtowel to put against his face. Gerald had never felt so ashamed, slumped against the wall, the man standing a safe foot from him until the police came.

The cops took him to St. Vincent's, where a doctor told Gerald he was extremely lucky to have his eye, but it would heal. No internal injuries that they could tell. He was tender and bruised all over; his knees were raw, and there were some welts on his back, but the main injury was on his face. The doctor was particularly concerned about his ear, which was torn half an inch off his head. He stitched and wrapped it thickly in gauze. His mouth was badly swollen with small cuts, but no stitches were necessary. "This'll hurt like hell tomorrow," the doctor said in a matter-of-fact voice. Marks from the chain, little oval circles, were etched across his cheeks in two perfect lines. His mouth, the concert. What about the concert.

"What do you do?" the doctor asked, as if reading his mind.

"Musician."

The doctor shook his head. "You look pretty bad," he said. He asked Gerald if he knew who the kids were, if he would recognize them.

"I don't know." The doctor shrugged, and gave Gerald a prescription, some special bandages and gloves to change the dressing, and an appointment card for a week later. He also gave him the name of a center where he could receive counseling and advised him to get someone to stay with him for a few days, that he shouldn't be alone. They had a protocol for muggings.

Gerald went home in a cab around 3 a.m., and hobbled up the stairs, each bend of the knee sending shooting pains up his thighs. There was a moment in the darkness of the entryway—he'd forgotten to put the light on before he went out—when he felt so suddenly frightened that he could hardly get the key in the door. "Wait!" he yelled at the cab driver, who had already backed down the street and couldn't hear him. He got in, finally, turned on all the lights and dropped the shades quickly. He poured a glass of orange juice, shaking, then realized he couldn't drink it. He would have to get some straws. Gerald fumbled with the bottle of painkillers and when he finally got it open the jar tipped and the pills scattered across the floor. One left. He couldn't swallow. Perhaps if he just left it in his mouth it would dissolve.

Music; he wanted some noise to fill up the bright quiet, but he couldn't think. He shuffled over to the machine to let whatever CD was in go on. He took a dish towel and laid down on the couch.

You make me feel so young…like spring…sprung. Frank Sinatra. Yes, he remembered. Stephen had left that disc in when he'd come by yesterday. He should call him. But it was the middle of the night. If he were well, if Stephen were well, Gerald would call him, but not tonight. He should call John. But no, he was out of town, wasn't he? Snatches of the evening at Stephen's flashed in and out like an old film. The thinning carpet, the screen-saver designs on the computer in the corner, the weight of Stephen as he leaned against him. "Yeah. Me, too," he'd said. Then the man jogging down the street, the sheen of his outfit. The damp air. He could only hear with the one ear, see the plaster-swirled ceiling with one eye. He was afraid to close his eyes; the scene lay just below his eyelids: the clinking snap of the chain, the dirty metallic taste, the wetness, the kid's black eyes.

You know what you are.

Would John have come?

Of course he would have.

Gerald sat up and began to cry. He cried, his mouth and eyes stinging fiercely, and then vomited into the towel. He cried for a long time, and then he was quiet, stiffening with pain. The CD player had long since gone off, and now the room was growing light with early morning. The light and the quiet were like the pain, encasing him, neutralizing everything. He felt he could have sat there the rest of his life.

Chapter 12

Gerald had told her to be there at nine to go over the music. She had sweet-talked her uncle about working, *again*, and now he wasn't even home. Where was he? His car was here, parked on the wrong side of the street for today, a ticket flapping under the windshield wiper. She'd been waiting ten minutes, long enough for anyone to finish their business and answer the damn door. Herminda knocked on Gerald's door one last time, this time with the base of her palm.

She had hauled her luggage tote back down to the sidewalk when the door opened. "What?" was all that came from her mouth at the sight of Gerald. His shirt was hanging out from his pants, stained brown and red and some kind of mustard color that could have been vomit. There were two purple lines on his face, as though someone had drawn little ovals across his face in lipstick. One line went along and over his mouth, which was swollen so badly he looked like a clown; the other disappeared in a diagonal under a bandage over his right eye. His left ear was swabbed in a huge bandage. Finally, she realized he was bald on top of his head; the toupee was missing. He was hanging onto the doorknob for support.

Herminda came up the stairs hesitantly, as though like some dangerous stranger he might reach out and hurt her. Gerald lifted his chin slightly toward the sidewalk where she had left her horn, and she ran back down and towed it back up the stairs.

Inside, Gerald grabbed her shoulder suddenly and leaned on her for support. His touch surprised her and she forced herself not to pull away. He was behind her in an awkward way; she couldn't get an arm around him and so they shuffled slowly that way to the couch, where he sank with a moan.

"Gerald, what happened to you?" She squatted in front of him. Her voice was scratchy.

Gerald lifted his hand briefly, but his lips were swollen shut and she could tell he wouldn't be saying much. Now he was moving his hand in the air as though he was writing, and she ran into the kitchen and found a pad and pen by the phone.

"*Mugged last night,*" he wrote with effort. "*Church St.*"

She didn't know what to say. He looked bad. Had an ambulance been called? She wondered why he hadn't been admitted to a hospital. Maybe she should figure out some way to get him to the hospital. 9-1-1? That might be a little dramatic. She could call Mickey; he could drive Gerald to the hospital. No, not Mickey. Not now. She didn't want him in *every* part of her life. She chided herself. If she could drive, *she* could take him to the hospital. Maybe Roland—he could drive Gerald's car, although she wouldn't know how to get in touch with him. Her mind was racing in circles when she should be doing something for Gerald. He was writing again.

"Should you go to the hospital?" she blurted.

"*Bathroom. Need help.*"

Oh, god. Would she have to go all the way into the bathroom with him? She didn't think she was up for this. She didn't want to touch him. What about the rehearsal Wednesday, she thought, suddenly—the performance?

"Can you walk with me? Can you make it there with me?" she asked. Her voice was not her own. It was clear and low, practically calm.

He nodded, and she squatted in front of him again so he could scoot over and put his arm on her shoulder again. "Put your weight on me," she said, "It's okay." He moaned as he stood up. The stretch from the couch to the bathroom door seemed like a city block. Herminda flipped on the bathroom switch, wondering what would be next. In all her visits, she had only been in the bathroom once before, when she'd stayed for dinner. It was a man's bathroom, all clean and uncluttered and done in navy and white, with dressing room lights over the long mirror. She knew Gerald had a cleaning service; no regular person kept a bathroom so clean. Her mind was wandering to keep from thinking about what she was doing. Should she stay in the room? She would have to stay. He couldn't lift himself up. How had he gotten to the front door in this condition? Would she have to take his pants down? Her palms were sweating.

"Okay," she heard herself say, "I'm just gonna turn around and wait here. Can you get your pants? Just tap my back if you can't." She crouched by the cabinet so that he could lean on her if he had to while he fumbled with his pants. He tapped her shoulder, grunting. She made a point of turning her head away as she unhooked his pants and zipper and pulled them down, gently, and went back into her squatting position so he could ease himself onto the toilet. He moaned as he pissed, and Herminda wondered if there might be something wrong inside of him.

When he was done, he tapped her again and she rose slowly with his weight and again turned her head as she pulled up his underwear and slacks and zipped them. He cleared his throat in thanks and they shuffled slowly back to the living room. His cheeks were wet when he sat back down; she could barely look at him. He was crying and she wanted to leave.

The phone rang and she jumped up to get it, eager to get out of the room.

"Hello?" she said.

"Ger? You sound strange. You want to go for breakfast before the appointment today? I'm starved. I was thinking all night of eggs benedict."

"This is Herminda Matta at Gerald's house," she said formally.

"What? Where's Gerald? This is Stephen, a friend of his."

"I just came for a lesson. He's been hurt—somebody mugged him. He's all banged up."

"Someone broke into his place?"

"No. Somewhere on Church Street last night, I guess. I don't know exactly when. He needs some help. He can't talk, hardly."

"I'm on my way," he said, and the phone clicked off. Someone else was coming. Herminda felt relief flow through her, and it was easier to go back into the living room. She sat down near Gerald, noticing a blood smear on the white leather of the couch. "That was Stephen, your friend," she said. "He's on his way over."

Gerald nodded. His cheeks were still wet. She didn't know what to do. She put her hand on top of his and they sat like that for several minutes.

When the doorbell rang, Herminda jumped to answer it. She recognized Stephen from the time they all came into the cafe a couple of months ago—a tall, pale man with a big nose and receding dark brown hair. He bustled in quickly, as though late, slinging his coat off awkwardly onto the floor. "I couldn't find my key, Gerald," he said, loudly, although he was facing Herminda. "I know I had one, though, and it was a pisser to get a cab. I don't know why." He rushed in, pushed the coffee table out of the way—she hadn't thought to do that—and knelt in front of his friend.

"Oh, Jesus fucking Christ, what did they do to you," he exclaimed, as if he knew the culprits. Herminda was embarrassed, watching Stephen run his thumb gently down Gerald's face, examining the little oval marks across his cheeks. She hadn't been able to look Gerald in the face since she saw him in the doorway. "Church Street? They jumped you on Church Street on the way home?" A slight nod from Gerald. "How'd you get to the hospital? Never mind. Which one? Saint V's?" Another nod. "Did they look at you for internal injuries?" Nod. "It looks like a chain. One of those sticks with a chain. Some of those fucks think they're fucking ninjas. Oh, fuck. *Fuck.*" Stephen pulled Gerald to him and held him gently.

"Are you hurting anywhere other than your face?" Gerald nodded. "All over, right?" Stephen smiled tightly. "Did you get meds? Where are they?" Gerald tilted his head toward the table by the window. There were pills scattered all over the table. Apparently he'd had trouble getting the bottle open. "How many did you take?" Gerald shook his head. "Two? Three? What? None? Oh, fuck, you can't even get your mouth open; how would you get something to drink? Oh, baby, no wonder you're crying," Stephen said, hyperactively heading into the kitchen. "Straws," he called. "Where are your damn straws?" Herminda came in to help him and they looked in every drawer.

"Look," he said to her, "I'm going to run down to the corner and get some straws. What else." He opened the refrigerator. "Some, like, Gatorade or something. Can you stay with him?

And I've got to go to my appointment. I can't miss it. I'll get straws and Gatorade and then I have to go for a while. I hate to put you out, but can you stay with him til around noon? I can't get back til then."

Herminda wondered what appointment this Stephen had that was so important but nodded. "Thank you *so* much," he said, touching her shoulder lightly. "What would we have done if you hadn't come by this morning?"

"Just going for straws," Stephen said breezily toward Gerald, grabbing his coat, "so we can get those drugs into you. God, what *is* that odor?" He stopped by the edge of the couch and picked up a towel and cleared his throat. "We'll just put this outside for now," he said, opening the sliding door, and Herminda realized the rank odor she'd been smelling was vomit. How like Gerald to find a towel to puke in, she thought.

Stephen was back in less than five minutes and he smashed a couple of the pills into a glass of Gatorade and had a straw up to Gerald's mouth before she knew what he was doing. Gerald moaned, but sipped the entire glass.

"Now to the bathroom," Stephen said, and Herminda sighed as if he'd read her mind, having to be with Gerald another couple of hours. She dreaded another trip to the bathroom. They were in there a long time, it seemed, and she stood by the sliding glass door and listened to the muffled sing-song of Stephen's voice and felt like crying herself.

Gerald seemed better when he came out with Stephen. "I think the meds are starting to kick in," Stephen said, his voice considerably less tense than before. "I put some ointment on his lips so they don't completely seal up. Now, to bed." Herminda followed them into the bedroom and stood in the doorway while Stephen helped Gerald ease back onto the bed, shifting a couple of pillows under his head. Then he untied Gerald's oxfords—didn't the guy ever wear sneakers? Herminda wondered—and covered him with a blanket. "Herminda is going to stay while I go to the hospital." Stephen brushed by her and came back with the pad and pen and a clean towel. He was a good nurse, she thought. Gerald held up a finger, scribbled a few lines, and passed the note to Stephen who passed it to Herminda.

Practice.

Herminda sighed. "Right." She waved her hand briefly in acknowledgment. Gerald was definitely coming back to himself.

She left the room to set up her horn and Stephen followed, leaving Gerald's door open. From the kitchen she heard him call a cab. When he came out he lowered his voice and said, "When I get back I'm calling St. Vincent's. There's blood in his urine, just a little. Something's banged up inside." Herminda nodded, putting her bassoon together. She appreciated the way Stephen talked to her like a friend, but she didn't know what to say back. She hadn't thought she would like him when he'd come bustling in, but he was a nice guy. She watched him put on his jacket and wondered if he and Gerald had been lovers.

"If you're thinking about the rehearsal, don't worry about it," Stephen said. "It's just a rehearsal. And Gerald told me you were really exceptional. You'll do fine." Stephen patted his pockets briefly, as if for cigarettes, and retrieved his sunglasses. "Well. I'll be back."

She liked to hear that Gerald thought she was exceptional. Herminda smiled to herself, forgetting for a moment as she put her horn together what had happened to Gerald. She would play the solo at the rehearsal. The thought made her stomach ticklish with nerves and excitement; then she felt guilty feeling this way at Gerald's expense.

It would be too strange to practice here in the white living room after all those sessions in the kitchen. She was uncomfortable at the thought of Gerald listening to her work on that solo.

The flat was quiet. Herminda tiptoed to the doorway of his room. Gerald was on his back and appeared to be sleeping deeply, his breath regular with a little humming noise, his lips glistening with ointment. There was a yellowish stain on the bandage on his ear, and she wondered how bad it was under the white gauze. Gerald's thin hand looked strange lying palm-up on top of the quilt like that, almost like he was dead. Herminda gazed at him and imagined what things would be like if he had died. She did not speculate why someone would do this to him; it was like the kids hanging out in the park—you could list individual reasons why each of them would hurt someone else, especially someone who had more, like Gerald—and all together that anger added up to more than its parts. It turned into something meaningless. Just violence, bad luck.

Herminda took her bassoon into the kitchen and closed the door behind her. She laid the horn across a chair, closed the drawers that Stephen had left open in his search for straws and put the Gatorade in the refrigerator. She wished there was something else she could do—some dishes, or mopping the floor, but the room was clean and orderly. She set up the chair and music stand as usual and began her scales.

Halfway through, not concentrating, her eyes filled with tears and Herminda didn't know whether she was crying because of Gerald or because she was afraid she was pregnant. She had managed the whole morning, getting here, and then Gerald, just thinking about the rehearsal, not dwelling on the fact that her period was a week late and she had never been late before.

She had thought she should get pills, like her sister, but Mickey said they weren't good for your body, and he would take care of things. And he had, mostly. They made love a lot and it was hard to remember. Maybe there were a few times. She had meant to go to the clinic and get an exam, maybe a diaphragm, but she had been afraid of the way they would look at her, how they might not believe she was really 20 years old. The whole thing sounded like one of those commercials on her mother's late-night television, and now here she was. And she was going to have to tell Mickey, and then what. What would she say? What would he do? What would he want? She remembered looking into the mirror before the first time they went out, wondering this. It was only a few months ago, but it felt like years. If she had a baby now…. She would have to tell him tonight.

Herminda stood up suddenly, laid her instrument down again and wiped her face at the sink. She tiptoed through the living room to Gerald's room to look at him. He was still on his back, propped up by pillows, but he had shifted slightly. His mouth was open and his breath was raspy, but it didn't look like he was in pain. She looked at the photo of John and him by the bed. He didn't have the toupee on then, either. He looked friendlier without a toupee. What would Gerald say if he knew she was pregnant? It would probably be the end of everything.

She called the produce shop and luckily her mother answered. "My teacher got mugged," she said, in Spanish, to increase her mother's sympathy. She couldn't explain Gerald or Mickey or much of anything these days to her mother.

"Are you gonna come in?" her mother responded in English.

"I don't know. I don't think so."

There was a clucking on the other end. "Well, José won't be happy. But I'll tell him."

Herminda went back to look at Gerald, who hadn't moved, and left his door slightly ajar and stood in the living room for a few minutes. It was now almost noon, and Gerald's flat was very quiet, unlike any time of day on Florida Street, where someone was always peeling out, or yelling, or slamming a door, or playing a boom box loud. She took a deep breath. She loved this quiet. She was going to get chewed out by her uncle, but it probably wouldn't be so bad since her mother was working this morning.

The solo. Herminda stopped the scales and pulled out the score for *Rite* from her folder. She had played the first bassoon part every time she'd practiced, but just for fun, not with the idea of actually having to play it. She went through the fingerings on the first page without blowing into the horn. The melody was in her head. She figured if she could get the first high F out smoothly, she could make it to where the second bassoon came in. She liked thinking of it as a sort of adventure, like crossing a river. Nothing mattered. She was alone; she closed her eyes. First F, her lips just so around the reed, just the right tightness for a high, extended note. It was perfect, clear; she could feel her body relax into the note, and then the solo followed almost as if the Fox were playing by itself.

She went through the solo and the rest of the first section several times. With only the bassoon sheet music to examine and what she could make out on the tape player at home, Herminda couldn't wait to hear how the rest of *Rite* would sound, with the other instruments filled in, first a faint bass clarinet and cornet underneath her, then the other bassoons, then the flutes... to be inside the piece instead of listening to it. She was fantasizing about this when someone cleared their throat behind her and she jumped, thinking Gerald had somehow gotten out of bed.

"Just me," Stephen said. "Didn't mean to be so quiet. I found my key. It was in my wallet, of all places." He took a bag to the counter. "I looked in on him," he said, tilting his head toward Gerald's room. "He's sleeping hard, which is good. I brought us some sandwiches if you're interested." He removed a couple of packages wrapped in butcher paper and took some plates from the cabinet.

"Sure," Herminda said. She had been practicing almost two hours.

Stephen pulled up a chair and sat down at Gerald's breakfast table. Herminda laid her horn across the empty chair and joined him.

"I heard a little of the solo, if you don't mind," he said, sliding a soda toward her. "It was nice. Very nice. *Rite's* one of my most favorite pieces of music. Berkowski's a bit of a grouch, but don't let him bother you. And Richard. You mustn't let him try and bully you into letting him play first bassoon. You've got it. Gerald wants you. Richard will, you know, bully you." Stephen had finished his sandwich and licked his lips, crumpling up the paper. She had only taken a bite.

"Sorry. I'm always voracious after my appointments."

"What are your appointments?" Herminda asked hesitantly.

He looked at her. "I have AIDS. Lots of injections at the hospital."

Herminda flushed. "Oh." She had imagined it was something like that, but she was surprised and embarrassed that he would say it.

Stephen laughed and patted her hand. "'Oh.' Now that's the right response. I mean it."

Herminda did not feel patronized by his comment. She knew Stephen liked her.

"Which all brings me to another subject. Ger needs someone to stay with him tonight, and I told another friend who's real sick I'd be there for him tonight. What do you think about Roland? He lives down from you, right? Do you think you could get him to come over for the night? Stop by his place?"

Herminda nodded. "Sure. I mean, I can try. If he can't stay, I will."

"You will?"

"Sure."

Gerald had not awoken when she left after lunch, heading home to drop off her bassoon. As she hoped, no one was around. Her mother would still be at the store. She called the shop and this time José answered. He was not impressed.

"I can find other girls to work for less," he said.

Fuck you, she thought.

If she went down to the house to leave Roland a note, she would be late for work at the café, too, and she called to tell the morning waitress.

All the shades were down at the house where Roland lived. Just last week at the café Roland had said the guy hated light, that the inside of the house was immaculately clean and all the walls had been redone, painted forest green in a Victorian style. Herminda knocked and waited, thinking of knocking and waiting at Gerald's—was it just this morning?—and no one came. She wondered where Roland would be. Work? His job at the brokerage ended around 2. It occurred to her that he might even drop by the cafe. She left a note with her phone number and it tucked into the doorway: *Roland, Call Gerald. He got mugged last night. Needs someone to stay with him. If you can't I will. Herminda.*

At the Cafe Del Sol, she was relieved it was Mickey's day off and that it was busy with no time to think about anything. She was supposed to go to Mickey's house after work for dinner and to stay over. She had slept over a few times before at his place in the big pull-out sofa bed in the living room. She liked sleeping together, waking up together in a big bed, not the narrow one she slept on most nights. They had made love each time in the early morning before they were completely awake, and Mickey's hands would be on her, large and warm, and sometimes he would massage her and sometimes he would tease her and sometimes they would just move toward each other. Each time she had made up the bed and left while Mickey was getting Christopher dressed.

Her body clenched thinking of those mornings. They weren't very careful then. It was a long bus ride to his house after work. She would have to get a test, probably from the drugstore. And talk to Silvia. Silvia would probably know what to do. But, then, maybe not. If her sister got pregnant, she'd probably want to keep the baby.

Mickey had made roast chicken and stuffed peppers. He was in a good mood, bustling around the kitchen, setting up Christopher with watercolors. Herminda could've helped more with Christopher, but she didn't think the boy liked her. In three months he'd never said hello; he always just looked at her and directed all his talk to his father. Perhaps he still thought she was the babysitter. She ate her meal in silence.

"Long day, with Gerald and all," Mickey said, cutting up Christopher's chicken.

"Yes." She had called Gerald's place before she left work. Stephen was still there. He said Roland had gotten the message and would be staying over with Gerald tonight, so that was not an excuse to leave. She finished her glass of wine. She wanted to go home.

It took almost an hour for Mickey to put Christopher to bed while she waited in the living room. He finally came in with the rest of the wine and their glasses and tapped the door shut behind him with his foot. He poured her a glass and sat down beside her on the couch. "Cheers," he said, and there was a feeling of familiarity in the way he said it that was like they were married.

She took a sip of the wine. "I'm late," she said abruptly, moving back from him. She forced herself to look at his face.

"For what?"

"My period is late," she said, flushing.

"Your period is late," he repeated, looking back at her, not comprehending for a moment, and then, slowly, a look of happiness came over his face, as though she'd just given him a gift.

"Minda," he said, putting his glass down. He pulled her close and held her.

Mickey's shirt was old and soft and smelled like him, like soap and a tinge of garlic. She wanted to cover herself with him like a blanket, but only if he felt the way she did and didn't want her to be pregnant.

He stroked her hair, then leaned over and kissed her lightly. His eyes were closed. "We can deal with this," he said, softly, after a few moments. "This can work."

"What do you mean?"

"I mean, we can do it. There's room here, and Christopher and I would love it if you moved in. You could have the baby."

"I could have the baby," she repeated.

Mickey smiled at her. "Yes." There was a new look on his face—no, not a new look, but one she had never seen directed toward her It was his fatherly look; she had seen it when he talked to Christopher, when he gave his son something he wanted.

Then he was holding her again, kissing her, and she could feel him wanting her, his hand on her hip. How could he feel like making love after she had just told him this? How could he?

"Wait," she said, pulling back. "How can you be sure we can do this? What about my...music?"

He smiled. "I don't see why you can't have a baby and still play bassoon."

"Yeah, and work two jobs? I can't do that."

"We can work something out."

"What if I don't want to?" she said, her voice cracking. "Have a baby."

Mickey looked as if she'd slapped him. After a moment he said, "You should have started with that, if you're feeling that way," he said.

"I don't know how I feel," she said.

This was not entirely true. All the past week, waiting, she had thought about it. She tried to imagine herself pregnant, like about a third of the girls who graduated or left school when she did. Working in the produce shop—full-time, probably—getting heavier and heavier. Silvia would be impressed. Her mother would not be happy about the fact that she wasn't married, but she, too, would be excited about a baby. And maybe it wouldn't happen immediately, but soon enough she'd stop playing bassoon. She knew this was true; there would be too much else to take care of.

"Well, I feel like...an idiot. You didn't think of me in all this, did you," Mickey said, as if following her thoughts.

"No, I didn't."

They were both quiet for a minute. Mickey had turned sideways to her now. He was leaning on his thighs and his hands were clasped tight.

"Well," he said, finally, "I guess I just wonder what that says about us. You and me. I thought we were...close. I know I love *you*...." He looked at her. His face was incredibly sad but the sadness scared Herminda rather than drawing her toward him.

"Do you love me, Minda?"

She bit her lips. She knew anything she said would be wrong, or not quite right.

"Well," Mickey sighed, "I guess that's enough of an answer. So. I guess I was someone handy... someone *safe* to have sex with. That's what I was." He gulped down his wine. "Although, I guess, not so safe." He made a sound like a chuckle and Herminda cringed suddenly at the way he sounded, the way the room felt. The plaid couch, Christopher's sneakers, Mickey's jacket, the southwestern style rug—everything in the room seemed strange and dangerous to her.

She stood up quickly to go, grabbing her jacket and putting it on almost in one motion. "Minda," he said, and took her hand. As earlier, she forced herself to look at him. His eyes were glistening. Until that morning with Gerald, she realized, she had never seen a man cry. And now here were two in the same day. He did love her, she said to herself, like a reprimand.

"I will call you. In a couple of days. After the rehearsal."

She walked home fast from Mickey's place to Florida Street, her hands in her pockets. The air was damp, chilly, but not yet foggy—a night like last night. It was probably around this time that Gerald got mugged last night. What was she doing last night? She had worked late, and her friend Clarice had called when she got home. They had talked a long time, about nothing. She had told Clarice nothing of what was happening to her.

He did love her, Mickey did; she knew this. He was so different than any men she'd ever known—her uncle, her brother, Gerald, that English teacher at Mission High. He was kind. He wanted to take care of her, and he wanted her to succeed. Or did he? Maybe he just wanted another baby. The thought made her cringe. How could he want a baby with her? Why did his love feel like a scolding? She thought back over the sequence of expressions: Mickey had gone from non-comprehension right to happiness. There had been no fear or dread in the middle at the idea that she might be pregnant, that she probably *was* pregnant, and for some reason she didn't like it that he was so happy, so quickly reconciled to this new situation.

On the corner of Florida and 23rd a group of boys was hanging out, passing a brown bag. She glanced at them and averted her eyes, walking quickly. There were a couple of jeers and then they went on talking among themselves. Herminda recognized a couple of them—Ricardo's sometime friends. If she were visibly pregnant, she knew, they would be respectful. Someone would offer to walk her home. She would be like a piece of community property.

Inside, the house smelled like *carne asada*, with a faint tinge of engine oil. Ricardo must be home. Herminda passed by the door to his room, which was half open.

Ricardo was passed out on his bed, one leg dangling off the bed. His jeans were dirty. In sleep a frown covered her brother's face, almost a boy's pout, but older now, more permanent. What was he dreaming of? His hands were gray with grease that wouldn't wash out, one across his chest and the other palm-up on the tousled bedspread, and Herminda thought of Gerald's hand on the quilt this morning. She imagined Ricardo dead and suddenly the dark room frightened her.

In her own room she turned on the small lamp and sat crouched on her bed with her knees up. She didn't want to think about anything. About Mickey, or Gerald, or what would happen next. She couldn't. Her mind flickered to her cousin Felix, suddenly, his weight on her six years ago. The smell of him, like the smell in Ricardo's room, that oil smell. She pulled the blanket around herself, shivering. She wanted out of this house, that's what she wanted. Now. Immediately.

There was a soft knocking on her door—how quietly Ricardo must have awakened and padded down the hall—holding the doorknob and knocking; she knew it was him. Had he been awake and seen her looking at him? She turned out the light. "Meanie," he said, loudly, and she froze. She was afraid of him, suddenly, just as she was afraid imagining him dead. But he was her brother; he wouldn't hurt her. That was Felix, not Ricardo, *Felix*.

"Meanie, can I come in?"

She swallowed and said, gruffly, "I'm in bed."

"I saw your light. Can I come in?"

"I'm in bed."

There was silence.

"Are you alone in there?"

"Yeah. Of course," she added, clenching her teeth.

"Well, hey. I wanted to tell you. I got a job for a while. Construction. Down near City College. Gotta fix up my car so I can drive down there."

"That's good," she said, loudly, her eyes squeezed closed. She pictured Ricardo leaning against the door, speaking to the crack, his palm against the wood.

"So. Maybe you want to go out soon? Maybe have a beer?" His voice, softer and sadder than she had ever heard it, frightened her. Why was she so frightened?

"Yeah."

"Okay," he said, and she heard the scratchy sound of his hand brushing the hollow-core door. Just as she'd pictured it. She turned on the radio low. It was a break; someone announcing something. No, someone was describing a cellist's debut. Get to the concert, she thought, stop talking. Stop talking. Finally, the music began, a cello solo, with a dramatic beginning, then a long, plaintive melody. She heard the shower go on in the bathroom.

Half an hour later she heard Ricardo's door close, and then the front door. He would be out all night again, she thought. She had to leave; there was a panic in her that was greater than the sum of its parts and she couldn't imagine sleeping in this room anymore.

She could go to Clarice's. In the morning she could call and make up an excuse. It would be chaos with Clarice and her boyfriend, but she knew Clarice would let her stay there a while until she found a place. Herminda looked around the porch that was her room and knew exactly what she would take with her and what she would leave. How quickly everything came to an

end, was changed, she thought—how quickly —and got up to
wash her hands.

Chapter 13

He was reduced. The word echoed in his mind: *reduced*. He made
a kind of mantra of it. He was vaguely aware of people coming
and going, of them stopping at his doorway to look at him. The
medication made him feel delirious, but for a while nothing on
his body hurt, specifically. He thought of shifting his position
but couldn't. Finally, Stephen came and took him to the
bathroom again, and the pain was back, his head and ear and
back throbbing. Stephen made him take a couple more of the
pills and helped him change his clothes and take out his contact
lenses, which were beginning to scratch his eyes. The medication
kicked in again as Stephen was leaving. "Roland's here," Stephen
said. "He's staying the night. You're not alone."

*You're not alone—you know what you are—*another mantra in his
head, punctuated by the sound of the chain coming around his
face. The chain wasn't hurting, but still he winced each time he
felt a shift in the air behind his head. *Kacheesh.*

"Gerald," someone said. He opened his eyes. The room was
dark; someone else was in the bed, and his arm was rigid,
clenching someone's hand. John. He wanted it to be John.
"Gerald, it's me, Roland. It's okay."

Roland, in his bed.

"Do you want the light on?" Roland asked.

"No."

"It's 2 in the morning. You're not supposed to get any more drugs until 3, but I'll give them to you now if you want."

"Thanks." He whispered. He rolled carefully onto his back. He didn't remember taking the last dose, or when Roland had come. Roland turned on the lamp on his side of the bed. He tapped out a couple of pills and put them on Gerald's tongue. Gerald attempted to swallow the water he offered, but most of it dribbled down his chin. Roland wiped it with a tissue.

"Did you get them down?"

He nodded.

"I'll just sleep on this side, okay, in case you need anything."

"Yes."

Roland, in his bed.

"They really beat the shit out of you," Roland said quietly, and Gerald wondered briefly if this was something Roland might have wished on him, but Roland was stroking his arm, gently, and he drifted back into sleep.

It wasn't sleep, exactly. The scene replayed itself over and over, the characters changing. *A bad movie*, someone behind him said, and chuckled. First, the chain coming across his face, a foot on his back. Screaming, his own. Pebbles in the street, pebbles grinding into his lips. He was going to die. They were going to kill him. He wanted to apologize. Then it was Herminda, suddenly tall and powerful, holding him by the collar. *You know who you are*, she said. Roland, behind her, laughed. And Stephen behind him, on the sidewalk, already dead. John was there, too, motioning to him to come and help. Stephen? he asked. The chain. He had to get to Stephen. John was trying to pick him up. The chain was coming at him from both sides. He could feel pieces of his face ripping off. An odd sound, like fabric tearing. He was going to die; it didn't matter. Boys yelling in Spanish. Then Stephen was gone; he'd been taken away, and he was sitting under that streetlight with the man, waiting for the police. He was trying to hold his face together, but strips of it kept slipping back into his hands. *My face, my mouth*, he whispered to the man, who was pacing, looking at his watch. *You're a fucking faggot*, the man said, his face suddenly his father's, shaking his finger at him. *Yes, yes, I am*, Gerald said, as if in admitting it the-man-his-father would help him put his face back on. From the doorway Gerald could hear *The Rite of Spring*, the solo. His face was wet. He was crying, or bleeding. *That's me, that's my song*, he tried to explain to him. *Goddammed fucking faggot*, his father said in a soft, almost pleasant voice, *I should finish you off*. He pulled a stick-and-chain from his pocket. The chain was very long, like a whip. *Please*, Gerald said. *Please*. The word was a yes and a no. Someone laughed. He felt himself piss his pants.

His eyes opened and Gerald sat up suddenly, ignoring the bolt of pain across his bruised side. The bed was damp, he couldn't tell from sweat or piss. He was wearing boxers, and socks, and a sweatshirt. Although the blinds were drawn, streams of light broke through at the corners. The apartment was quiet; his ear was throbbing; where was everyone? Had they all gone? Was he alone? Was Stephen dead? He had the feeling that Stephen was dead and he began to cry. By the time he got to the door and across the living room he was crying loudly, a strange wheezing moan. The door to the kitchen swung open, and he saw Roland, and beyond him Herminda was sitting with her bassoon assembled across her lap, her mouth open in surprise.

"*Geez*, Gerald, like, ask for some help," Roland said, quickly efficient. He slid himself under his arm and took him to the bathroom, talking the whole time. "You were really out, so I let you be. I should've woken you up, probably. Over here. Lean on the counter. Let me help you down. Geez, Gerald, do you have to do every fucking thing yourself?"

"Stephen," Gerald said.

"He'll be over after lunch. You can have the whole afternoon with Stephen."

"You sound...like him," he whispered.

"Great. Now are you going to finish pissing or do I have to do it for you?"

Gerald took a breath and looked at himself in the mirror for the first time, his vision blurry. His hair was matted, and his bare scalp was crisscrossed with scratches. The right side of his face was purple; and two sets of darkening purple ovals crossed his face. His lips were swollen, the bottom one split. The bandage on his ear made him look like a clown. He put his hand to it, then sat back down uneasily on the toilet seat.

"Colorful, huh," Roland said. "You don't want your glasses to see *that*. Stephen told me I should hunt for your glasses." Roland was running water in the sink, waiting for it to get warm. Gerald watched him as if he'd never seen him before. Perhaps he hadn't. Roland was nervous.

"Let's get some of those crusties off before you get up," Roland said, as if to a child. He was living with someone who was sick, Gerald remembered. Someone who was dying? He couldn't remember. Did he wash that man's face, he wondered, as Roland gently dabbed at his eyes and lips and cheeks. "Stephen said not to touch the bandage." Roland took some ointment from the counter and rubbed it on Gerald's lips. Gently. Gerald watched the tip of Roland's tongue poke through his lips in his concentration. "There." His mouth actually felt much better. He could open it and it didn't hurt so badly.

When they got to the bedroom, Herminda was changing the sheets. She had put on an old set that he hadn't used in a long time. "Clean sheets are good," she said awkwardly. He nodded. She left the room, and Roland helped him into clean shorts and sweats and a fresh sweatshirt.

"Do you want some drugs now? Some breakfast?"

"Coffee."

"Coffee. With a straw. Okay. No pain-killers?"

Gerald shook his head. Not now.

Roland went to make the coffee. Herminda came to the doorway and stopped there suddenly, as if surprised to see him sitting there on the side of the bed. He felt her looking at him, and he met her eyes for a moment. He was scared again, suddenly, and felt himself tremble.

"I need to find my glasses," he said. "Maybe they're in that table."

Herminda came over and knelt by the nightstand. "These them?" she asked, pulling out a pair of wire-frame aviator-style glasses. She tried to put them on him, but the bandage was in the way.

"Later," he said, raising his hand. She folded them back into the case.

"You're on...your own tomorrow, you know," he said, carefully. His mouth was hurting.

She nodded, standing in front of him, uncomfortable.

"Well." He had nothing else to say. He wanted her there, but he didn't want her to look at him.

The room was quiet. Roland came in with a tray, poured some coffee efficiently and knelt in front of Gerald with the mug.

"My father was an old man, a long time before he was old," Gerald heard himself say, from nowhere. Herminda glanced uneasily at Roland.

"You're not at work," Gerald said to Roland gruffly.

"Playing hooky."

"Thanks."

"Oh Jesus, Gerald, don't thank me. Just don't thank me, okay?" Roland stood up. He was still holding the coffee for him.

Gerald closed his eyes again.

Roland touched his arm and then he heard him leave the room.

"Did you want me to play any of the stuff for you?" Herminda asked suddenly.

"Yes. That would be good," Gerald said, his throat was raw. "Maybe...you could bring the stand in here. Do it in here."

Gerald arranged himself carefully back into a reclining position on the bed. He heard Herminda and Roland talking quietly in the other room, and then Roland stuck his head in and said, "I'll give you a call, okay? I can stay tonight if Stephen can't."

Gerald nodded and did not say thank you. He heard the front door close.

Herminda brought in the stand, and her horn. She settled herself nervously and played a couple of scales.

"Don't worry, I won't stare at you," he said.

"What?" She stopped, anxious.

"I said," he sighed, "I won't stare at you. I can't see anything anyway. So," he took a breath. "Just play like I'm not here." Talking was wearing him out. He took another sip of the cooling coffee and closed his eyes again.

Herminda finished warming up, and then went through all the rehearsal pieces, playing the first bassoon part. She must have been practicing the first part, he thought, as well as her second. Of course, she was a good reader... Normally he would be playing the other part with her—that's how they would practice for a performance. She must have played half an hour before she got to *Rite*. Just the bassoon part of the score, her foot tapping lightly on the bedroom carpet through the rests. His hearing seemed more acute even with the mangled ear. The notes circled the room clear, intense, as though he hadn't heard them before, but also completely familiar as if he were playing himself. Listening so still in the bed, eyes closed, drifting but also awake, Gerald imagined his cells realigning themselves, quickening then stalling, quickening. How strange this familiar body, the familiar sounds.

She came in on the solo perfectly, cleanly, so delicate. She was playing at least as well as he'd ever played it. He pictured Berkowski's raised eyebrows, the other woodwinds giving her the side-glance. She would do fine. His skin prickled. It was like hearing it for the first time and it *was* sweet. He opened his eyes, squinting at her, her mouth tight around the reed for the high notes. She held the bassoon like it weighed nothing.

What had happened to that singing teacher of his father's? Long dead now. The room rented, probably, dusty and empty.

Herminda stopped suddenly as Stephen poked his head around the corner and put his hand lightly on her head. She smiled self-consciously. "No worries about her, eh, Gerald? I let myself in..." Stephen was saying, cheerily, and then something snapped; a sob rose through Gerald's body and he began to cry and couldn't stop.

"I told Herminda she could take your car to the rehearsal tomorrow," Stephen said loudly, over the noise of the water rushing into the tub. He dramatically poured some dishwashing liquid into the water. "A bubble bath is what you need," he'd said after he changed the bandage on his ear. "Juicy," he commented, examining the stitches. Gerald had kept his eyes closed, concentrating on Stephen's presence close by. Stephen capped the new bandage with a plastic bag.

"Okay, Bozo, into the tub." He helped Gerald ease into the warm water. He rolled a towel up and placed it beneath his neck.

"You've got this huge beautiful tub and no bath pillow and no bath oil. I can't understand you sometimes."

"I never take baths," Gerald whispered.

"Well, there's your problem. You probably thought that women take baths; men take showers. Do you mind?" Stephen gently took Gerald's hand off his forearm.

"Would you...sit over here?" Gerald asked.

"What, on the floor? Well, okay. Your floor's a lot cleaner than mine." Stephen propped himself up against the tile wall and put his forearm on the side of the tub again so Gerald could put an arm on top of his.

"So, anyway, I told her to take the car, and I gave her the keys. I even gave her a little list of things to pick up on her way home." Stephen snickered.

"I didn't know she could drive."

"What?" He shrugged. "Well, she took the keys like she knew what she was doing." He paused. "So much for that car." He chuckled again.

"Did you tell her...to go in the back way?"

"I told her to get there early, and go in the back way, and find a grouchy looking guy with a big mustache. I called Berkowski anyhow and told him. He wanted to know, of course, whether you'd be out of commission for the performance. I said, 'We hope not'. I told him you'd talk to him in a couple of days. He said he was sorry. Etcetera."

"I could've called Richard to take her."

"Oh, leave Richard out of it. I can't stand that guy. So squirrely."

"One could say the same about you."

"Yeah. Who's talking." Stephen leaned over and shut off the water. "If there's still blood in your piss tonight I think you should go in tomorrow."

"Okay."

The bathroom was steamy now, and the sound of the water lapping in the tub was soothing.

"And I think, if you're not in pain, you should lay off the medication they gave you."

"You think I'm getting strange?"

"The drugs make everyone wiggy." Stephen smiled. "I think you scared the shit out of Herminda."

A flash of panic rushed through him and Gerald clutched Stephen's arm again. "What if you're the one I love?" he said, hoarse.

Stephen pivoted suddenly on his butt and sat cross-legged beside the tub. "Honey," he said, "I *am* the one you love. Look at me."

Gerald felt like a child. He looked at Stephen. His eyes were so gray and luminescent that they looked almost silver. Was it his vision, or was Stephen going, was he dying, was this like a mirage? He blinked.

"I mean, what if you're the one I'm in love with. In love with you. After all this."

"Well. Wouldn't that be something. But Ger, I don't think so. I don't think you've ever wanted to make love with me, and I gave up on you a long time ago. I'm kind of a short-timer that way, anyway. Remember the old days? But I know you love me. And I love you. I do." He took Gerald's chin and turned it toward him. His eyes scanned Gerald's face. "And if you weren't in such a… vulnerable position, I'd tell you how ugly you are."

"What about later, when you're gone?"

Stephen dropped Gerald's hand.

"Gerald. Would you quit enacting my own death for me? Okay? I'm well for now. You could've died the other night. We could both be dead. We will both die. Jesus Christ, I feel like I'm high school. With Andy Cavanaugh. We both wanted to fuck and we ended up talking about how we would die.

"The point is," Stephen took Gerald's chin again, pinching it so it hurt, "the point should be very clear to you, dear, is right now. Participation. Now. Everyone's here for you. You should be here with them."

Stephen squatted next to him alongside the tub for another minute. "You're going to get cold. Let's get out." He helped Gerald up, dried him off, and pulled him close to him with the towel and held him for a long moment. Gerald could smell him through his shirt, a little bit of sweat and something pungent, like ginger. He took a deep breath.

"Roland's coming again tonight. He said he'd make dinner. He's a good cook, you know. And," Stephen took a breath, "I called John this morning. He'd just gotten back from his trip. I didn't know what kind of a place you were in with him so I told

him to come over tomorrow sometime. That's okay, right?"
Stephen kissed his good ear.

"Okay," Gerald said. "Okay."

Chapter 14

After she heard Ricardo leave, Herminda had put the items she would need in a large green plastic trash bag, including some clothes and her tape deck and tapes, and lay awake on her bed until there the light through the bamboo shades changed and was gray. It was 5 a.m. The house was as quiet as she'd ever heard it. Her mother must have clicked off the television. She suddenly found it hard to believe that both her mother and Silvia were sleeping only yards from her and imagined the distance over and again as if there were not walls between them. From the kitchen, Herminda called a taxi for the first time in her life. Fifteen minutes later, as the cab pulled away from the curb, the bag of belongings and her bassoon taking up the back seat, she looked out the window at the house where she had lived for the past eight years, the weathered, rickety front porch where the light had never worked, a little box of darkness in the early morning gray, and she felt relieved. She would not be living there anymore.

In the taxi it occurred to her that Clarice and her boyfriend might not appreciate being awakened or surprised by her plans to stay with them until she found a place. She would have to call Clarice to arrange it, later in the morning. She gave the driver Gerald's address. Roland was staying over with him, she remembered, and she could make her arrangements there.

At Gerald's, she put her belongings down and sat on the stoop for a while, surprised at the quietness inside herself, and at 6:30 she knocked on the door. After another minute she knocked again and finally Roland opened the door. "Can I come in for a while?" Herminda asked, picking up her bassoon case, and he let her in.

Roland was wearing only a tee-shirt and boxer shorts and looked tired. The sofa bed was open and the sheets were disheveled. "I thought you were Stephen," he yawned. "What time is it? Are you okay?" he asked, eyeing her, and she nodded. He paused, but didn't ask anything else, and she appreciated it.

"You can go back to sleep, you know. I'll just go in the kitchen. I'll be quiet."

Roland yawned. "Maybe I will, for a little while. Gerald seems okay."

In the kitchen Herminda washed her face in the sink. She hadn't thought of Mickey since she'd called the cab. She hadn't thought of being pregnant, either, since last night. Did she look the same? She touched her throat. Her heart was pounding. She had to keep a hold of everything now and not panic. She would make breakfast and at 9 o'clock she could call Clarice. That would be late enough.

Herminda set out two plates and knives, made a pot of coffee and sat down at the table as though she visited Gerald's every day. After a while she heard noise in the living room and Roland joined her, wearing a bathrobe this time. "Couldn't sleep," he said, pouring coffee. "Actually, I'm kind of glad someone else is around," he said.

"How is he?" Herminda realized she was afraid to see Gerald now.

"Well, he woke up in the middle of the night grabbing my arm." Roland shrugged. "I gave him some more drugs. I don't know if he was hurting or not, but he was freaking out a little. For Gerald, anyhow."

Herminda put in some toast and they had breakfast in silence like siblings who ate together often. She kept waiting for Roland to ask her why she'd come over, but he didn't. She looked at her watch, feeling a bit guilty to be using Gerald's place as a base of operations while he was injured.

"I'm moving out," she said finally. "I'm going to find my own place."

Roland appeared unsurprised. "That's a good idea. I've always kind of wondered how you could live with all those relatives."

Herminda cringed when he said *all those relatives*. Perhaps Roland thought she lived in a house with three or four screaming infants.

"On the other hand, I've never had any relatives to live with in the first place—other than Gerald, who's a relative of sorts—so my opinion doesn't count." Roland got up to put another piece of bread in the toaster. "So where are you going to look?"

"I don't know."

"The Mission is the cheapest, but maybe you'd get lucky. Especially if you rent with someone. You kind of have to, don't you, so you can get a place where you can practice?"

What Roland said was true; Herminda hadn't thought that far ahead. All she knew last night was that she couldn't sleep there anymore; she had to get out. She was suddenly very tired and would have liked to collapse on the bed in the living room and let everyone just go about their business while she slept. She got up from the table to call Clarice. The phone rang several times but no one picked up. Herminda couldn't remember if Clarice had an answering machine.

Roland was watching her. "You know, you *could* stay here— tonight at least. I'm sure Gerald wouldn't mind. I'd still stick around. That's what you should do."

It was a relief to hear someone say confidently what she should do. Perhaps for one night it wasn't a bad idea. The rehearsal was tomorrow.

"I've got to practice," she said suddenly. Practicing would steady her. "Will I wake him up, do you think?"

Roland shrugged, opening the morning paper. "He's been out for about 7 hours now. I'm sure somewhere in the back of his mind he's worrying about the rehearsal, and if you're here maybe he won't worry so much." He smiled at Herminda's look of relief. "Of course, maybe he'll worry even more...."

She threw a damp dishtowel at him.

Twenty minutes later they heard a noise in the other room and when Roland swung open the kitchen door to the sight of Gerald crying in the other room, Herminda felt like she had melted and then froze. And later, practicing in front of him, surprised at her own lack of nerves, at her own intense involvement with each note she was playing, Herminda felt the same way when Stephen came in and Gerald began crying again in a way that made her tremble. A kind of melting and freezing, a breaking-down and resolution, then another break-down.

After that, she left. Stephen had mistaken the green plastic bag of her belongings for trash and had put it at the curb. She retrieved it and quietly put it just inside the door and went to work at the produce shop. She worked wordlessly with her mother all afternoon, who asked no questions about where she'd been—she probably hadn't noticed Herminda had left, since she rarely looked in her room—and tensing up only when she saw a tall man with red hair enter, but it wasn't Mickey. Herminda would have to tell her mother what she was doing, but later, after the rehearsal. She managed to reach Clarice, finally, after several calls.

"I'm moving out," she said bluntly, "and I was wondering if I could stay with you guys for a couple of weeks or so." She was at a public phone outside the produce shop and could barely hear Clarice. There was a long pause.

"I... that would be really fine if it was just me, Minda, but Stefan's got a friend staying with us here already, and there's not much room, but you could leave your stuff and all."

Herminda sighed. Now she did feel like crying; she felt she might burst. Stefan was mean, she thought. He was mean like Felix, and there Clarice was and she probably did everything Stefan said. And "their" place would fill up with his friends, and her belly would fill up with his baby. This was unfair, since she'd never even visited them since they'd gotten the apartment. "Okay," she said, softly, "never mind."

"What? I can't hear you. Why do you have to move out all of a sudden?"

"I just do," she said. Of that, at least, she was certain.

There was a pause. "Well, why don't you come over? Have dinner or something? We could go out."

"I can't right now. I've got to find a place."

Herminda hung up and went back to work, tired and edgy. She didn't have a plan, and she needed one, but she couldn't think. After work she walked for a long time, hands in her pockets, clenching and unclenching Gerald's car keys that

Stephen had given her to take to the rehearsal tomorrow. She stopped and ate a taco, and finally went to a movie to keep herself from arriving back at Gerald's too soon.

At 9 o'clock Roland let her in again. Other than insisting that he take the sofa bed, they didn't talk. She worried a little about Gerald finding out she was staying at his place, but she was exhausted and fell asleep quickly on cushions on the floor to the muted flickerings of the television. In the morning she got up very early and took a shower. She hadn't thought ahead as to what she should wear to the rehearsal and ended up with a pair of wrinkled black slacks from the plastic bag and a cotton sweater. She dressed quickly. She did not want to see her body in the mirror.

There was a knock on the bathroom door, and Roland said, "I guess I'm going to work today. Gerald was asking about you. I told him you were already here, that you'd come very early." He chuckled outside the door. "Anyhow, there's breakfast. You should eat, and early, so you don't barf it all up in nerves. Good luck," he added.

Alone at the small kitchen table again, eating some cereal, Herminda realized she was more nervous about getting downtown than she was about playing. She certainly couldn't drive, and she didn't know what prompted her to take Gerald's keys from Stephen. If Roland had been there, she would've asked him to drive her. She decided to call a taxi.

She heard a noise and scooted back in her chair as Gerald pushed open the swinging door. He had put on a bathrobe and was looking more normal. His mouth was still swollen. The bruises across his face had softened, and his whole face had a bluish-yellow tint, but his eyes were recognizable. The past couple of days it seemed he'd been gone. Now he seemed almost back in his body.

"Hello," she said.

"Could I have some coffee," he asked from the corner of his mouth.

She jumped to pour him some. "Do you need a straw?"

He shook his head.

"Roland went to work today," he said.

"Yes."

"Good." He sipped the coffee carefully. Herminda realized she liked his hair better this way, all pointy and unkempt in a ridge around his skull, and the small, bare top—although the skin was scratched and red right now.

"So you're on your own," he said.

Herminda hesitated. Had Gerald figured out that she had stayed over the past two nights? "Yes," she said.

"Well, you played...beautifully... whenever it was. Yesterday? You'll do fine." He paused. For the first time it occurred to her that Gerald might be thinking she would play better than him on that particular solo, and she smiled at the possibility.

He put his hand across the table toward her. She hesitated again, then put hers in his.

"Thank you," he said. "I'm going back to bed. I don't feel quite as strange as yesterday. No bad dreams." At the door he turned. "You know where you're going and everything, right?"

Herminda nodded, suddenly energized. She got up to help Gerald to bed, but he held his hand up. "I'm okay," he said. So she cleaned up the breakfast dishes and waited for a little while until she thought he was asleep, and then she called a cab.

She told the cab to pull up in back of Davies Symphony Hall, on Franklin Street, as Stephen had instructed. The driver watched quizzically as Herminda unloaded her horn and pretended to know where she was going. She was almost an hour early. The parking lot was nearly empty, and she wondered if the doors would be locked. She found a blue door marked "Musicians", which opened to a long corridor of doors on each side—practice rooms, she supposed—and then a double-door marked "Instrument Room." The lights were on, but no one was in the room. There were chairs and padded benches scattered all around, like an upscale locker room, the wall lined with black cabinets. Herminda put down her horn and walked slowly around the room. She found the cabinet marked "G. Poulin", unlocked, as Stephen had said it would be. There was nothing inside, not even an extra case of reeds. If it were her locker, she thought, she'd have some extra reeds, and a spit rag. Maybe even extra clothes. She took off her jacket and put it in.

"Can I help you?" a man's voice said sternly, and she turned suddenly, swallowing. It was Gertz. "Oh, it's you," he said. "I'm so sorry; I forget your name."

"Herminda."

"Herminda, yes. How is Gerry? I've been meaning to call, but I didn't want to disturb him."

"He's better." She didn't know how much to tell him.

"That's good. I *will* call him. Well, it's good you're here, then."

"Can I warm up somewhere?" Herminda asked.

"Well, sure. You can warm up in here—that's what most of us do. Or I suppose you could even go onstage, but it's a little early.... oh, Andrew!" he called suddenly to a big man who had just passed down the hall.

The man stopped, his belly shaking with the movement of turning toward them. He was bald, with a shaggy white mustache, and was wearing a white shirt with thin red stripes and blue jeans. His eyes were intensely blue. "Andrew, I want you to meet the bassoonist who will be sitting in for Cynthia. Or, actually, Gerald. She played in that little production I ran for Berkeley this winter. Herminda...." He mispronounced her name.

"I'm Herminda Matta," she said softly.

"Andrew Berkowski." He put out his beefy hand and smiled at her. His gaze was straightforward and friendly, not assessing, and Herminda felt a sense of relief. She'd thought the conductor would be more condescending, more like Gertz. "Gerry has recommended you. Always room for a good bassoonist with Stravinsky." He chuckled. "How is Gerry? I talked to Stephen Greenberg on—when was it—Monday, and he wasn't too hot."

"He's better," she said again. Berkowski looked at her as if he expected her to say more. "He's a little freaked out," she added, wincing at how stupid that sounded.

"Yes, I'd think he would be." She felt Berkowski was scrutinizing her. "I was planning on visiting him tomorrow. Do you think he'd be up for that?"

"Yeah."

"Good." He smiled and pivoted, then turned halfway back. "If you need anything, or have questions, Gertz here can help you. And—what's-his-name—Richard and Leonard, will be here soon."

Gertz smiled weakly at her. "No need to be too nervous. He's really a rather nice person. And he knows you're filling in."

Herminda felt a sudden urge to surprise them all. Berkowski was probably chuckling at her.

"Thanks," she said. "I guess I'll maybe just put my horn together and go out to the stage. Could you show me where to sit?"

Gertz led her down the corridor to a door, and then down another short hallway to the side entrance to the stage. The lights in the theater were on low, but the stage lights were bright.

"Here's the bassoon section," Gertz said, indicating four chairs. "Gerald, Cynthia—er, you —, Richard and Leonard."

"Thank you again," she said stiffly. She followed him back down the hallways to the instrument room. There were several more musicians in the room now, many giving her a quick glance, pretending, she thought, not to stare. She smiled bleakly at them, quickly assembled her instrument, and took it, the music folder, her rag and box of reeds to the stage. Best to sit alone on stage than worry about those people staring at her.

Alone on stage, next to Gerald's empty chair, she began to warm up right away, her eyes closed. If she sat still in this large auditorium she knew she would get nervous. After a few scales her horn was warm and she opened her eyes. Someone had turned down the stage lights. Herminda saw someone look at her from the hallway and turn away. She could not play the solo, or any of the music. She didn't want anyone to hear her. She'd have to count on her good luck of the past morning.

Slowly the musicians trickled on stage. Herminda was completely alert now, hardly able to sit still in her seat, watching all the musicians in their street clothes warming up, thumbing through the music, and chatting with those to either side of them and behind and in front of them. How familiar they all seemed to each other, she thought. She pretended to look through her music. Some just looked at her, a flutist smiled and asked how Gerald was; most appeared not to see her at all. The other two bassoonists were among the last to appear. Herminda recognized Richard from the time Gerald had invited them to play duets together, and Leonard, an older man, heavy, with white hair introduced himself just before Berkowski came on stage. Herminda saw Alec Coughlin rush in from a side door and fumble to get himself set up. All voices stopped when Berkowski stepped up onto the podium and clicked his stand, like a priest about to begin a Mass.

"It appears Mr. Coughlin, our prodigy, needs a few more moments to get settled," Berkowski said, and there were a few chuckles. She saw Alec's face redden. "So, while he is readying himself, I will get myself a chair." Berkowski stepped off the stand, and the chatting started up again immediately.

He came back with a high stool which he placed very dramatically on the wooden podium. Once again, everyone was quiet. Herminda was slightly embarrassed, watching Berkowski lift his heavy body onto the stool. He seemed to move extra slowly so that everyone would watch him.

"Most of you may have heard," he said, "that Gerald Poulin was mugged over the weekend and injured especially on his face. His ear was almost torn off his head." Berkowski voice was angry and disgusted. Herminda wondered what the muggers would think of him. A murmur went through the musicians; many of them looked at her. "However, it appears he will be back possibly as early as next week. And so," he said, turning toward Herminda, "we are grateful to have a student of his, Herminda...Matta... to fill in on first bassoon for him today. And when Gerald comes back, she will be sitting in for Cynthia."

She felt all eyes on her. He had pronounced her name perfectly.

"Okay, let's get started," Berkowski said, shifting his weight. "We've got three pieces—three easy pieces—" he chuckled at the grunts from his orchestra, "Oh, just *kidding*—you folks are so *serious*—we'll start off easy, with the Rossini." Herminda opened her folder like everyone else, grateful to begin with the piece that had the least bassoon in it.

"I'd like to at least get *through* all of them this morning...." Berkowski flipped through the stack of scores on his stand. "We'll see." He clicked the stand as if to get his own attention again. "Howard?" he said to the first oboist, sitting a couple chairs away from Herminda. Everyone brought their instruments into position to tune, and the oboist's *A* was gradually drowned out. It was a relief to Herminda to blow a note and feel some of her nerves loosen.

The Rossini went quickly. They stopped twice, and when the Overture was over Berkowski said, briefly, "Not bad. *Bolero.*"

Herminda's heart was throbbing in her throat. She hadn't thought much about *Bolero*, but the first bassoon started off the piece with a solo. There wasn't time even to run through the fingerings. Berkowski clicked the stand again, and everyone stopped. "Howard," he said, and this time the oboist played but no one joined in. "Herminda?" Berkowski said, and she tuned in with the oboist. Then he pointed at Richard, and Leonard, who joined in. Then, as if joking, Berkowski pointed at each woodwind player until they were running out of breath. He stopped them with his baton. "Okay?" He tapped out a pace for two measures on his stand, then brought up the baton, and Herminda heard herself begin the solo, trying to see both the notes on the score and Berkowksi's baton from the corner of her eye. Then she heard Richard coming in with her, and then the cellos were plucking out the rhythm, and then she heard the snare drum from the corner of the stage, and then the whole orchestra was playing. She was surprised at how easily they went through the piece. It was common enough, she knew, but she still didn't expect so many of the musicians' faces to have such a look of complacency, of normalcy. If she had a job playing for the symphony, would she become that way, too? Berkowki caught her eye and smiled. She'd done all right, and she hadn't even worked hard on that piece.

After one pass through *Bolero*, they took a short break. "And I mean 5 minutes," Berkowski growled, again as if angry, but smiling, and he lumbered off the stage. Howard the oboist looked over at Herminda and smiled primly. "Nice job," he said.

"Herminda," Richard said, struggling over her name, and she turned to face him directly for the first time since the rehearsal began. "I don't know how you feel, but if you're at all uncomfortable with that solo that starts *Rite*, I'd be glad to fill in. I've done it many times, actually."

Herminda remembered Stephen's warning.

"I think I'm okay," she said. "I'd like to give it a try."

Richard shrugged, and got up abruptly. Herminda felt her palms begin to sweat. Her underarms were soaking, she realized. A line of perspiration was dribbling along her forearm where the sweater ended.

She stood up to stretch and glanced over her shoulder. Alec caught her eye and smiled. Then she heard a clapping and Berkowski was striding across the stage again. "Okay, everyone!" He waited until everyone was settled. "Enough of this. Bassoons. I must have more bassoons." Berkowski looked at the three of them over his reading glasses, which he had put on by the end of *Bolero*, and squinted at them doubtfully, but still smiling.

"Are you ready?"

Herminda felt her throat squeeze so tight she didn't know how she would pull out the first note.

"Herminda," he said softly, again perfectly, "can we hear the opening, say to the 2/4?"

The orchestra was quiet. Beside her she heard Richard lick his reed and blow gently through it for a second. "It's only a rehearsal," she repeated to herself, and her mouth clamped down on the reed to make the opening high F, and then she heard it come up slowly, gradually, singing through the whole horn. The note unleashed her and she wasn't afraid; she followed the score as if there were nothing else in the world for her, and when she was done, when she got to the place where the second bassoon came in, she stopped. It was absolutely quiet for a second on the rehearsal floor, and then Berkowski said, "Yes. Very nice."

Some members of the orchestra chuckled at the understatement. Herminda felt goosebumps rise all over her body at the praise and felt a line of sweat trickle from her forehead. She dabbed at it with her rag.

"And so might I just ask one question?"

Herminda bit her lip. What could he ask her? She didn't know if she could speak.

"Where have you been, Herminda Matta?"

The orchestra laughed. No answer was expected, she realized.

"So, shall we proceed?"

This time Berkowski held his arms up in readiness to draw the rest of the orchestra in. Herminda felt braver. Richard came in after Letter 3. The piece took up the rest of the hour and a half; Berkowski stopped and started the orchestra several times to go over rhythm sections, and to clarify to himself how he wanted to conduct the piece. Gerald had told her Stravinsky's piece was probably more difficult to conduct than to perform.

The symphony had done it several years ago, but since then there'd been a lot of personnel changes.

Berkowski ended the rehearsal ten minutes early. He closed his book and said, quite deadpan, "I have to take my daughter to her piano lesson."

There was a general amused murmur. He pursed his lips, evaluating the rehearsal. He wavered his hand in the air. "So-so," he said. "*Rite* will be our focus next time. Violins, we're going to take care of that problem? Hannah," he said to the first violinist, "perhaps a sectional? Everyone else, next week, same time. Bernice has some papers for you on your way out." He swiveled on his chair and lumbered off toward the offices. A couple of musicians walked alongside him to ask him questions, scurrying to keep up.

It was when she stood up that Herminda felt the familiar gush from her body. "Where's the bathroom," she said abruptly to Richard, who pointed down the hall. She laid her instrument across two chairs and practically ran. Maybe all this time she was just late. She couldn't stop trembling, and when she put her hand to her face her cheeks were wet with tears, although she didn't feel like she was crying. She took deep breaths, relieved.

When she came out another woman was there. She hadn't heard her come in. Herminda washed her face quickly.

"Hi. I'm Helen Kraut," the woman said, turning to her. "Fourth cellist." She was young, petite with short curly hair, jeans and a black tee-shirt. She extended her hand. Herminda wiped her hand on her pants and shook the woman's hand limply. "That was beautiful, that solo."

"Thanks."

"I don't mean to embarrass you."

"It's okay."

"I bet you get teased a lot for playing bassoon. Being small, and all. I know I do. My brother-in-law is always making jokes about getting something so big between my legs. Etcetera."

"Yeah. It's pretty heavy." Herminda couldn't think of anything else to say.

"Actually, Alec mentioned to me that you might be interested in doing a jazz group with us. Him, and me and a friend of mine who plays sax."

"He did?"

"Yes."

"Well, I'm not together right now. I mean, I don't have a place to live and some other things."

"Well, you can come and check it out any time. We're not starting up til summer."

"Great. Thank you, for telling me."

"Will Gerald be back next week?"

"I think so. I hope so."

"Well," she put her hand on Herminda's arm, "nothing at all against Gerald, but you did great on your own. Berkowski doesn't say 'very nice' very often."

Herminda smiled. She wondered how long Helen had been in the Symphony. She was relieved that almost everyone had cleared off the stage by the time she came to retrieve her bassoon. It lay across the two chairs, bocal stem up, as if relaxing. She sat down carefully in a chair beside it. The Fox had done well by her. She smiled again. For the first time, she could look around the auditorium, rows and rows of seats rising and the acoustic panels angled this way and that like rudders up and down the side aisles.

This was a place for her, she thought. She might not have known that if Gerald had been here today, coaching her, telling her what to do. She would have liked to tell somebody this. Mickey, perhaps. Certainly he could understand that she would want this. She would have to call him. She remembered what he said about no room for him. That was possible. It was possible there was no room for him, that he was too old or she was too young. She didn't want children now. Maybe never. She felt like she could *think* now, at least, now that she knew was not pregnant.

"Admiring the view?" Alec said, leaning cross-armed against a beam by the backstage curtains.

She smiled. "Yeah, I guess."

"I was wondering where you were. Helen said she'd seen you. Wiped out?"

"Yeah."

"You did fine."

"Thanks."

"You were all the talk in the instrument room."

"Well, I'm glad I didn't go in there."

"They're mostly gone now. You can go in."

"Okay."

"So you think you might be interested in a little jazz combo?"

"Yeah, maybe. I've just moved out. I have to find a place to live, maybe another job." She shrugged. She stood and picked up her horn. Alec escorted her to the instrument room. There were a few pockets of musicians still talking. She dismantled her horn and swabbed it out, not looking at anyone.

It was after 2 when a cab dropped Herminda and her bassoon and three bags of groceries off at Gerald's place. Alec had given her a ride to the store. She was getting pretty good at calling cabs, too, she thought.

She knocked, and Stephen answered.

"We were beginning to wonder what happened to you," he said. He took the groceries from her and took them to the kitchen. Gerald was sitting on the couch, and the man John—she recognized him from the picture—was sitting next to Gerald with his arm around him.

"So, how did it go?" Gerald's voice was almost normal.

"Good, I think. Yes, good."

"Berkowski called, actually," Stephen said loudly from the kitchen. "He said you were 'more than competent.' He has such a way with words."

"I was pretty nervous."

"Yes.' Gerald smiled at her. He seemed so mellow; she wondered if he was taking the pain medication again. She missed the tense edge.

"I'm glad it went well. Hopefully, I'll be with you next week. From the way Berkowski sounded, maybe *I* should play second."

She smiled and covered her mouth with her hand.

"Did you like it? Being there?"

"Yes."

"Thanks for buying the groceries!" Stephen called. "We got a little worried when we saw the car was still here."

"I don't drive that well, yet," she said, huskily.

"Well, look," John said. "Sit down, relax. Have some lunch. You must be starving."

"Actually, I'd like to change. I'm supposed to be at work at 4," Herminda said, remembering her slacks and realizing suddenly that the plastic bag of her clothes was opened alongside the couch.

"Speaking of which," Stephen said, coming into the living room, pointing to the bag, "Is this stuff yours? I almost threw it out."

"I know. I brought it back in."

"What's going on, Herminda?" Gerald asked.

Herminda swallowed. She might as well just finish everything off today.

"I'm moving out."

"What?" Gerald leaned forward. "Did you get kicked out?"

She winced and closed her eyes. "No. I just had to. I guess I was wondering...hoping...I could stay here for maybe a week or so until I can find a place to live."

Stephen and Gerald looked at each other. John was looking directly at her.

"Of course," Gerald said. "No more questions. You can sleep on the couch."

"If Roland was here for six months, honey, you can certainly hang out for a week or two," Stephen said.

"Shut up, Stephen," Gerald said, a bit of the regular, sharp voice coming through.

In the bathroom someone knocked briefly and then slipped her package of pads through the door. Stephen. Herminda felt a wave of embarrassment, and then she laughed. Here she was staying in a house full of homosexual men. She looked in the mirror. Was this the same person from last November? She put her fingers to her face. Her skin, her whole body, completely different. Everything was changing.

Chapter 15

After five weeks, he had begun to mark time by the mugging. *That was before....* he thought to himself while making dinner or boarding a bus. Time passed in a kind of haze, an inertia, that Gerald had never experienced before. His body was healing but it didn't seem to be his. At times he tried to make himself go through the experience again, to *look it in the face,* to try and understand why it had happened to him, and if not *why* then what it would mean to the rest of his time. But always something would distract him—music coming from the house behind his, the sound of a woman's voice and the slam of a car door—and he couldn't think. He found himself in front of the television in the day and left it on even when he wasn't watching.

The hardest time of the day was in the morning, alone in bed, realizing John had gone to work. Gerald's throat would tighten, knotted in a kind of grief, and so he'd taken to getting up early with him. John had stayed over every night. Gerald wanted him nearby. Neither of them talked about how it had been between them before the mugging. Sometimes, looking at him, Gerald would feel like asking him something, but it would be a vague question like *What do we do?* and so he didn't ask. He felt as though he was stepping into the outline of his life, a peculiar theater and play for which he didn't know his lines. John demanded that he get out of the apartment, that he *practice* going out in the world, and although he could not bear to visit anyone, when John suggested a movie or a walk Gerald did not protest.

Both John and Stephen had suggested that he see the counselor the hospital had recommended. Gerald went twice, feeling a shell of responsibility toward his friends. After a description of the mugging, the counselor, a gay man, seemed more angry than Gerald felt and even seemed upset at Gerald for not being more angry.

"You probably should have seen a straight, corporate type. A woman therapist, maybe," Stephen said one evening when he joined John and Gerald for dinner. "You don't need anyone appropriating your feelings."

"But I don't feel *angry*," Gerald protested.

Stephen shook his head. "Well, I find that... unbelievable. You just don't know how you feel."

Gerald grunted. Who was appropriating what now? It was the first time they had talked openly about the mugging, all three of them together, and he didn't feel like listening or responding.

"Maybe it will take a long time," John said suddenly. "Maybe all this will just take a long time for you to feel like...anything." This was not the sort of thing John would normally say; it sounded almost like another person and Gerald was grateful, because it intimated that John would not leave him for a while. He looked closely at John's face—for the first time since the beating, he realized. He had been afraid to look closely at anything. John's eyes were sad and kind at the same time, with things withheld. Six months ago Gerald would have winced at the kindness and been concerned about the sadness. He knew that if he couldn't rise out of this inertia, John would eventually have to leave. But now he was simply glad John was beside him every night.

Since his mouth was healed enough, Gerald had practiced, but there was no natural movement through the work and he had to force himself to concentrate. He'd sat alongside Herminda for three rehearsals, listening to her play his parts, making suggestions, feeling like an athlete who'd been benched, only he couldn't sit along the sidelines; he had to take his place mid-court. It was uncomfortable—excruciating, even—but he was part of the team; he was responsible, ever-responsible, and when John drove him home each rehearsal he was more tired than if he had been actually playing. This morning's rehearsal was the first time he had been able to play. As he twisted on his reed and warmed up, he knew the others were looking toward him with a scrutiny they hadn't before—*will he be okay?*—a kind of expectation he hadn't experienced in a long time. When the rehearsal was over and the other orchestra members came up to him to shake his hand or say a few words, he was not sure whether it had gone well or not, although Herminda, beaming beside him, visibly relieved, had said it was fine.

He was not comfortable driving and had taken to riding the bus for his errands when John couldn't take him. There was something reassuring about people going about their business, getting from one place to another and not paying attention to each other. Gerald took care not to let his glance rest on any particular person, or he might begin to contemplate that person's life, too. *Why was that woman wearing a neck brace? Had she been in an accident? Had someone hurt her?* He would look away, back to the window, out at the street, at the progression of 24th Street: mothers pushing toddlers in strollers; men smoking outside a newspaper shop; two teenagers washing a plate glass window; a homeless woman rolled up in a sleeping bag in front of the laundromat.... and then the gradual change.... a bank; young couples with sunglasses sipping cappuccino on the sidewalk; a shop selling Balinese jewelry; organic produce in custom-made bins next to the wine shop.... If he'd gone this far, Gerald had missed his stop and he would get off and walk back to Noe Street and make his way home. He felt a new, resigned patience watching it all. Before, he would have seen the couples having cappuccino and contemplated getting off to have one himself. The liquor store would remind him that he wanted a bottle of Merlot for dinner. But now, from the bus, he just watched.

After the last rehearsal he had gone home in a cab (Herminda declined to share it with him, saying she had to go to work), and made a small lunch. Then he took the bus to get his slacks altered. There were numerous tailors on 24th Street, but Gerald had patronized one small shop not far from the hospital ever since he first came to the city. He'd lost weight in the last month. John had started to tease him about it a couple of times and then stopped. He wished Stephen and John and Herminda didn't have to feel so uncomfortable around him. Even Roland, on the visits he now made weekly, was careful. As his body recovered, there was like a plexiglass barrier around him, worse than ever. They were out there. It wasn't them he couldn't feel; it was himself. How many years of therapy would it require to feel that self again, he wondered—the pleasure of being in himself, of desiring something, of offering something, of doing something well.... He couldn't imagine. He would have even been grateful now for an outburst like the one in the tub when he had told Stephen he loved him. But the experience of healing had dulled him.

The bus back going west on 24th Street was full and Gerald had to stand. His mind wandered as he stood, braced by the overhead bar. The performance was tomorrow night and instead of the usual confidence and focus he felt before a concert he felt restless and uneasy. He wished it were over. So he could go back to.... what? It had crossed his mind a couple of times in the past week that perhaps he should leave the Symphony. And live on.... what? It was more than a pleasure; it was his livelihood—now *that* was an interesting word, *livelihood...* His mouth was a little sore from the rehearsal this morning. It would take a while for his jaw muscles to fully recuperate.

And then he saw him, two rows ahead. Gerald recognized him first by a feeling that tingled up through his gut and chest as he examined the young man. Gerald could see the collar of his red flannel shirt. He was slouching in the window seat, shoulder-length black hair tied back into a small ponytail. *Wait,* he thought. *This is ridiculous. Unlikely.* He had to be careful of these kinds of feelings, which might put him over an edge to which he already felt too near. But then the kid rubbed the back of his neck and Gerald felt the tingling again. The other kid he might not have known, but this was the one, the one with the club and chain.

The bus came to a stop and two people jostled by Gerald to get to the back door. He watched the kid glance impatiently at the people moving down the aisle, then turn his gaze back out the window. Gerald stepped up one seat so that he could continue to look at him. *I should be afraid,* he thought, but it wasn't fear he was feeling. He stepped up to the row where the kid was sitting. The kid glanced up at him and away.

Gerald looked at him and could not stop looking. It was the most peculiar feeling he had ever had. *What was his name?* He stared at the kid as if some vital information could be absorbed: the loose jeans, slender fingers stained with grease, a tendril of black hair curling down his neck where it didn't fit into the rubber band. If the kid jumped up suddenly with a knife that would be the end of him, but Gerald didn't think he had a knife, didn't think he'd use it on a crowded bus, didn't *care*. If Gerald had had a weapon himself, he wouldn't have been able to use it.

"What are you *looking* at?" the kid said finally, angrily, turning toward him to confront him, but the sentence was hardly out of his mouth before Gerald could see recognition blanching in his face. The kid turned sharply back toward the window, his hands clenched.

Gerald continued to stare and stare, fiercely, helpless to do anything else. His vision had never been so clear. As he stared he could see small beads of sweat popping out on the young man's neck. He felt the people around him tensing up and he could sense the rushing thoughts of his assailant—his *assailant...* If Gerald could stand there a little longer he would be able to smell him, to say his name, even.

Say it. *Say it.*

"Ricardo," he whispered hoarsely, the name that had been called out in the street that night. Then the bus began to slow down and the kid jumped up and slipped under Gerald's arm swiftly, without touching any part of him, and was out the back door. Gerald could see him running down 24th, lithe and quick.

Gerald got off at the next stop and made his way to a bench in front of a savings bank to sit for a moment. Although his heart was pounding, he felt strangely calm. *I have seen my assailant....* he thought, and the words reminded him of something he had read once. His eyesight was still exceptionally clear, and he watched the people pass by with interest: a red-haired woman pushing a baby in a stroller; two attractive young men with their arms around each other; an older woman that Gerald recognized from

John's office. It was better; something was better; he was released, for now, at least.

He realized how close he was to John's office. Just one block away, upstairs at his desk shuffling papers probably, his *lover*, and Gerald imagined John's face clearly, its thick, fading handsomeness, and decided he must go see him, right now.

Chapter 16

The Rite of Spring was the last piece of the concert. Berkowski had lifted his baton and gave Gerald the eye. They were all at readiness, Herminda and Richard and Leonard and himself, like a little musical corps, their reeds to their mouths, their aim in sight, and as Gerald came in on the high F, he had a surge of fear that something terrible would happen—his reed would split; he would faint.... and then he passed from the first bars and felt Herminda and Richard come in with the triplets beneath his notes, and he was out of danger. A slow smile spread across Berkowski's face as he caught Gerald's eye and nodded.

The rest of the 33 minutes went smoothly, beautifully. Gerald and Herminda only glanced at each other, but he felt her confidence beside him. The rehearsals on her own had indoctrinated her. After the performance Berkowski congratulated her, and she struggled not to beam. Gerald heard Pamela Miller, the first flutist, tell Herminda about a possible bassoon part opening in the Bay Area Women's Orchestra—a pittance, but a paying job. "I just heard about it today," Pamela was saying. In her black dress Herminda looked older, graceful in a way Gerald had not seen before. Tonight she would think about the performance, he imagined; it would feel like a dream, like everything was ahead and time was rolling out in front of her.

Watching her talk to Pamela, he knew they would have to cut back their lessons; it was time. Herminda had found a basement room in a house in the Sunset. She had her own entrance and access to a little kitchenette. "I can practice any time!" she'd exclaimed, since the older couple who lived upstairs were both hard of hearing. Herminda had also quit her job at the produce store. There had been several family arguments, and finally her mother gave up. Herminda had given her two tickets to the performance. Stephen had worked on a part-time job for her in the Box Office. That job started next week.

A tall man with red hair—the one she had kissed in the cafe—Gerald wouldn't forget him—came into the instrument room escorted by a security guard. Herminda came up and took him by the hand (a bit awkwardly, Gerald thought) and introduced him to Pam, then turned and scanned the room until she spotted him.

"Gerald, I want you to meet Mickey. Kelly. Mickey Kelly."

Mickey extended his large hand. "A pleasure. I've been hearing about you for months. The concert was great."

"Thank you." Gerald smiled. He felt at a complete loss for conversation. John and he had planned a party after the concert, and Roland and John had left immediately after the concert to set up. "We're having a little soiree at my flat, and you're welcome to join us," he said.

Behind him Herminda winced briefly. Obviously she hadn't mentioned the party to him. Mickey's face flushed, but recovered quickly. "No, thanks, I should get home to my son. Glad, finally, to meet you."

Herminda walked him to the door, holding his hand, and Gerald pretended to smile at someone across the room while watching them in the hallway. They were turned toward each other, standing close, and he was saying something. Herminda listened, looking hard at a spot on the floor, and then she looked up at Mickey and they embraced. Mickey kissed her on the forehead and she stood in the hallway alone for a moment after he left.

Gerald tried to turn away, but Herminda caught him looking and came over. They stood side by side looking at the spot in the hallway as though Mickey were still there. "He still loves me, he says," Herminda said abruptly. "He says there's nothing I have to *do* about it." She shrugged. "But I feel like I *should* have to do something about it, you know?"

He knew. Was this the same girl who came to his doorstep just over a year ago?

Gerald had invited Richard and Leonard and a couple others to the party, and they came and went quickly. It was more intimate now, the way he preferred it. From the kitchen where he and John were preparing the food, Gerald watched Roland serve Herminda a glass of wine and say something to her, nudging her as he sat down on the arm of the stuffed chair, and they both laughed. Alec Coughlin was behind them and laughed, too. Alec had convinced her to play bassoon in his rock band. Just last week Herminda brought him a tape Alec had loaned her, and Gerald was surprised to find he liked it. They had put the tape on and were listening to it. A bassoon or two might fit well into the things Alec was doing with rhythm.

The man Roland was renting from had died. His lover had put the house up for sale but allowed Roland to continue living there cheaply until it was sold. Roland had already made a new project of trying to convince John to buy it.

John came up alongside as he surveyed the scene in the living room and put his arm around him. Earlier this evening, Gerald had called him and asked him to drive. "Are you sure? John asked. "I don't want to get to the door and have you all in a snit like you usually are before concerts."

"I won't be in a snit." He recalled watching John's nostrils flare with the effort of properly finishing his bow tie.

"Gerald, please stand still. I'll never get it right if you keep twisting your head," John had said, and Gerald closed his eyes while he tugged. That close, he could smell John's aftershave— something John never overdid—but since the mugging all smells were more pungent, as if his olfactory nerve had been unhinged somehow. He had never been quite so calm before a performance as he had been tonight. He knew that nerves were required to keep an edge, especially with the solo, but right then he had just enjoyed the smell of John's aftershave.

There was a brief knock at the door, and before anyone could get up Stephen let himself in, followed by a tall, handsome man with thinning brown hair who looked like he might have been a model ten years ago.

"Hello, all. We thought we'd check in." There was a murmured hello before the guests turned back to their conversation. "Gary, this is Gerald, my oldest friend in the world —and I mean *oldest*... and John...."

Gary laughed nervously and brushed his hand on the leg of his suit pants before taking Gerald's hand. So this was the man Stephen had told him about, the one from the support group. "How do you do?" Gary said courteously, clearing his throat. He might have been about 35.

"I was going to tell you about him," Stephen had said last week when they were at the hospital for his appointment. "That morning when you were mugged. And then there was no chance. It's love again, thank god, of some sort. He thinks I'm incredibly funny, and smart, and even sexy."

"*Well*," Gerald said.

"You could do better than *well*, my darling. You could say, 'I'm happy for you'."

Gerald had turned to him in the waiting room, took Stephen's face in his hands and kissed his forehead. "I'm happy for you," he said.

"That's better."

Roland was reading excerpts from the program notes. "Okay, listen to this," he said and read an unintelligible paragraph about young forces, "implacable wise elders," ritualism, and predetermination. "Excuse me, how about a little English? This program could use a little clarity, if you ask me."

"The music was wild, Roland," Stephen explained. "Wild for then, wild for now. And so it's strange to think he was portraying the so-called 'unchangeable cycle'." Beside him on the couch, drink in hand, Gary smiled uncertainly.

"Well, take me out to the *wild*-erness, then, Stephen. Did you write these notes or something?"

"He could, you know," Gerald said.

"Well, what do you think, Stephen? Do you think everything is predetermined?"

Gerald could feel John tense up behind him in anticipation of an uncomfortable conversation.

Stephen smirked. "I don't know, Roland. Possibly. Probably. I don't really care, as long as the music stays wild."

Gerald took out a plate of melted brie with almonds and apple slices. "We should probably worry more about the 'implacability of the elders'", Stephen said, poking Gerald in the leg.

"Ah, the wise, implacable elder," Roland said, smirking. "Hey, Gerald, don't you ever serve anything tasteless-but-tasty, like those little pigs-in-a-blanket?" he asked.

"I don't understand a word you guys are saying," Herminda said, smiling quietly. She had had a couple of glasses of wine.

"That's lucky for you, Herminda," said Gerald, "and as for you, Roland, your hotdogs are in the microwave right now."

"Speaking of wise elders," John said, from behind him, "Just look at what came out of your broom closet, Gerald." He was carrying a big chocolate cake (they must've hid it in the oven) and everyone began singing Happy Birthday. It wasn't that he'd forgotten his birthday tomorrow, but he hadn't let himself think of it. Fifty-two marked no particular place, although 52 candles were enough to illuminate all their faces in the now-darkened room, like a medieval painting—a strange, unrelated group.

Everyone was laughing at the frosting-drawing on the cake of Gerald playing the bassoon. "I never claimed to be an artist," Roland said, "and of course your head *gleams* so much these days, it's hard to get a good perspective...." Gerald laughed and put out his hand, and Roland took it.

Herminda gave him a new seat strap for his bassoon; John gave him a sweater and a bread maker; Stephen gave him a ream of composition paper; and Roland gave him two tickets to an A's game. After the presents it was late. With much exclamation and laughter, Stephen and Gary went home. Both Herminda and

Roland were wired, and they sat up with John and Gerald for another piece of cake.

Afterward it was late, almost midnight, and Gerald was tired. John had already gone to bed. "But your feelings *will* change," Roland was saying to Herminda, a bit drunk, and Gerald left them for bed, unsure whether they were talking about love or work or music at this point.

Their lives were spreading out, Gerald thought, easing into his bed. Herminda was trying to be responsible; she eyed her new responsibilities with passion and he wouldn't meddle with that. Even Roland seemed less scattered. They were young. Gerald didn't know whether they would all remain connected. It was probably the wrong question. Hadn't he asked himself which love would last and which wouldn't, and what he would do when it was over?

Here he was, in his middle age, more grateful than hopeful. Since Roland, he'd tried too hard to stay in the middle. He'd let his feelings for John rise too slowly and settle too quickly. Perhaps in old age he'd become wild with hope; he didn't know. Beside him John snorted a little and rolled over onto his side.

It was late. In the other room, Herminda and Roland were still talking, and for a moment, like a parent, he wondered how they would get home, going opposite directions. Would they share a cab? Then he remembered Roland had a car now, and he let himself drift off to the sounds of their voices rising and falling, almost like a song.

Acknowledgements

When I first made this book by hand in 1998, I thanked many people, including my husband John, friends Paul Murray and Helen Fremont, and the Warren Wilson community of writers for their support and encouragement, and for being passionate readers. I also expressed gratitude to the Connecticut Commission on the Arts for support in completing the book. All of those acknowledgements also stand today, as well as thanks to Barbara Mariconda for some keen-eyed editing, and to all the folks who read and appreciated that "first edition." Thank you all, again.

About the Author

Virginia Weir grew up in the Southwest, graduated from San Francisco State University, and completed an MFA in fiction from Warren Wilson College. Throughout a life of writing, she has worked as a typesetter, database administrator, grant writer, and fundraiser. She lives with her husband in Connecticut. www.VirginiaWeir.com